"Reese, I'm sorry about what happened before."

Gabby looked into his eyes.

He frowned at her. "You mean...after I went into the service?"

She nodded and swallowed hard. "Something happened, and I couldn't... I couldn't keep the promise I made."

That something being another guy, Izzy's father. He drew in a breath. Was he going to hold on to his hurt feelings about what had happened?

Looking into her eyes, he breathed out the last of his anger.

"It's understood."

"Thank you," she said simply. She held his gaze for another moment and then looked down and away.

It had been so long since he'd been part of a real, good family that he'd forgotten he wanted it. Tonight, with her family, made him realize how much he wanted one of his own.

But in the back of his mind, a voice of caution warned. She'd already broken his heart once before. He shouldn't get too close again.

Lee Tobin McClain read *Gone with the Wind* in the third grade and has been a hopeless romantic ever since. When she's not writing angst-filled love stories with happy endings, she's getting inspiration from her church singles group, her gymnastics-obsessed teenage daughter, and her rescue dog and cat. In her day job, Lee gets to encourage aspiring romance writers in Seton Hill University's low-residency MFA program. Visit her at leetobinmcclain.com.

Books by Lee Tobin McClain

Love Inspired

Rescue Haven

The Secret Christmas Child

Redemption Ranch

The Soldier's Redemption
The Twins' Family Christmas
The Nanny's Secret Baby

Rescue River

Engaged to the Single Mom
His Secret Child
Small-Town Nanny
The Soldier and the Single Mom
The Soldier's Secret Child
A Family for Easter

Visit the Author Profile page at Harlequin.com for more titles.

The Secret Christmas Child

Lee Tobin McClain

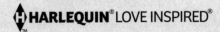

Recycling programs
for this product may
not exist in your area.

LOVE INSPIRED BOOKS

ISBN-13: 978-1-335-47958-7

The Secret Christmas Child

Copyright © 2019 by Lee Tobin McClain

This edition published by arrangement with Love Inspired Books.

® and TM are trademarks of Love Inspired Books, used under license. Trademarks indicated with ® are registered in the United States Patent and Trademark Office, the Canadian Intellectual Property Office and in other countries.

www.Harlequin.com

Printed in U.S.A.

For I will turn their mourning into joy.
—*Jeremiah* 31:13

To Dana R. Lynn and Rachel Dylan

Chapter One

"I'm not working for Reese." Gabby Hanks shook her head as she put the dinner tray she'd prepared beside her grandmother's bed. "No. Uh-uh. No way."

Nana shifted Gabby's nine-month-old daughter, who'd started to fuss, in her arms and clucked her tongue, and little Izzy's frown turned into a smile. One that matched Nana's persuasive smile all too well, despite the seventy-five-year age gap between them. "I'm making you a good offer. A place to stay, free childcare and a job that's right across the backyard. Which would be a real convenience, considering that heap of junk you're driving."

Despite her grandmother's brusque tone, Gabby heard what Nana wasn't saying: she herself needed help, even though she was too proud to ask for it. A bad case of the flu had left her weak and shaky. She shouldn't be alone right now. "We can stay here for a few weeks, until Christmas," Gabby said.

"And you can help Reese until Christmas, or at least interview for a position there," Nana said. "I happen to know he needs seasonal help."

"Nana. Why would an after-school program for at-risk kids need seasonal help?" Gabby pulled a second threadbare blanket over her grandmother's legs and looked anxiously out the window at the low-hanging clouds. The northern-Ohio wind whistled through the old, poorly insulated house.

"Because those kids' needs don't just go away when school lets out for Christmas break," Nana said. "Reese has an overload of boys whose parents work long hours and can't supervise them, so the church board is sponsoring his Christmas Camp." She picked up a piece of toast and bit off a tiny corner. "Thank you for fixing me dinner, honey. It's real good."

"You need to eat more." Her grandmother was way skinnier than she should be, and Gabby's heart constricted with guilt. Yes, she'd had to take a job on the other side of the state to pay her and Izzy's bills, but she should have visited more often.

A moot point now. She'd lost the job because of missing too much work; a single mom didn't have much choice when her baby was sick and she had no friends or relatives in town.

Nana's casual revelation that she wasn't feeling too well and "wouldn't mind a visit" had come as a blessing. Now it looked like the blessing went both ways.

"Anyway," Nana said, waving a hand toward the field that adjoined their edge-of-town house, "Reese's main assistant had to leave for a family emergency. He's in a spot."

"I'm sure there are plenty of applicants." Who *wouldn't* want to work with the second-most-popular former football player in Bethlehem Springs?

First most popular, now.

"You forget what a small town Bethlehem Springs is," Nana said.

Oh, no she didn't. That was a good part of why she'd left.

Bethlehem Springs had been a wonderful place to grow up, and most people had been kind despite Gabby's shaky family history and thrift-store clothes. She'd had a good life here with Nana. Firm friends, good grades, plenty of opportunities.

But that had all changed after the accident.

She sat down on the edge of the bed and held out her hands for Izzy. "Come on, let me hold you while Nana eats," she said. Gabby repeated her mantra: Izzy's what's important.

I'll take care of you. I'll do right by you.

Izzy was her joy out of sorrow, and she gave Gabby's life purpose and meaning. No, Gabby wouldn't have the caring family she'd dreamed of growing up, or at least, she wouldn't have a man to protect her; her dreams of a white knight had turned to dust. But she'd give Izzy a sense of security. That was paramount.

"It's a real godsend, your being here." Nana dutifully forked up a green bean. "I've been wanting to get to know my great-granddaughter."

Gabby patted her grandmother's thin arm. "I'm so glad we'll get to spend Christmas together."

And one of the first orders of business was to decorate. Normally, by December 1, Nana would have had the entire house decked out in red and green. The fact that there were no Christmas decorations out said it all about how sick her grandmother had been.

The doorbell chimed through the little house. Izzy yowled her indignation at the unfamiliar sound.

Nana set aside her plate and held out her arms for the baby. "Get the door," she said to Gabby, then pulled Izzy to her chest and made soothing noises at her. "It's okay, sweetie. You're okay."

Izzy quieted instantly, and Gabby smiled her thanks before heading toward the front door. Nana truly was a baby whisperer, and it would be wonderful to have her help with Izzy.

Not if the price was working for Reese, however. That, she couldn't tolerate. There was too much history between them, too much pain.

Nana's cat, Pickles—so named because of his sour disposition—sneaked toward the door, barely visible in the front room's dim light.

Gabby was wise to the feline's tricks. "No, you don't," she said, sweeping the cat into her arms. "It's too cold for you to go outside, and you're too old to spend the night out, anyway." As she spoke, she opened the door.

Reese Markowski stood on the porch in the winter twilight, a bag of groceries in one arm.

"Oh…" Gabby took a step back, sucking in a breath. She hadn't seen Reese for well over a year. His hair was shorter—the military thing—and his shoulders seemed broader.

And he had no smile for her now.

The cat screeched in her arms and she realized she was squeezing him. "Come in," she said to Reese, but the words came out in a croak, and she cleared her throat and repeated them, holding on to the struggling cat. She stepped back farther, the cat providing a convenient barrier.

Reese stepped inside and shut the door behind him,

and she let the cat escape, watched it stalk off behind the couch. She'd rather look anywhere than at Reese's eyes.

"I didn't know you were here," he said stiffly. "I was at the store. Brought your grandmother a few things."

"I can take them. Thank you." Although that would involve stepping closer to the man she'd once loved with all her now broken heart.

"I'll put them in the kitchen. Heavy bag." He walked past her without a second glance.

Clearly he felt at home in Nana's house. How long had he been helping out her grandmother this way?

And then realization came crashing in: he'd find out about Izzy.

She couldn't bear that, couldn't bear his questions, whether spoken or unspoken. She needed time to figure out how to present the facts of the case, how to frame the reality that she'd had a baby less than nine months after he'd left for the service. She hurried after him. "Thanks. Nana's sleeping. I'll take care of these from here."

"I usually put them away for her." He'd set the bag down on the counter and was shifting cans into a cup-board.

"It's not necessary."

"I can do it." His voice was sharp. "I still have one good hand."

Only then did she notice he was using only one hand for unloading the groceries. She couldn't see his other hand beneath his jacket.

"Did something...happen?" she asked.

"IED explosion. Amputated below the elbow." He used his left hand to flap the other jacket sleeve back and forth briefly before going back to shelving gro-ceries. The sleeve was empty.

She sucked in a breath and searched his face, taking in his tight jaw, the way his brows drew together. So that was why he hadn't finished his tour of duty. "I didn't know."

"There's a lot you don't know."

"But you were going to be a carpenter. Can you still…" She trailed off.

He shook his head. "Not the way I wanted to."

Pain wrapped around her stomach and squeezed. All his dreams. All that talent. Automatically, her eyes went to the cherrywood display case he'd made her, still in a place of honor on Nana's kitchen wall, holding her high school treasures—a trophy from a cheerleading competition, a silly clay figurine she'd made in art class, a photo of her and Nana on graduation day, Gabby's cap knocked askew, both of them laughing.

The case was beautiful, a work of fine craftsmanship that many men twice Reese's age couldn't have produced.

When she turned back toward him, he was looking at the display case, too. His lips tightened. "Don't waste your pity on me. See to your grandmother. She's not doing so well." He turned on his heel and strode out of the house, letting the door slam shut behind him.

Gabby wrapped her arms around her middle and stared after him, her heart twisting with so many emotions she didn't know how to begin to process them.

Reese had lost part of his arm serving his country. He could no longer do the thing he loved best.

Nana was sicker than she seemed.

Also, even before learning about Izzy, Reese seemed to hate her.

* * *

The next morning, Reese walked into the rehabbed barn that housed his program for at-risk kids, still trying to recover from the encounter with Gabby.

He'd made a fool of himself, not that it mattered. Acting touchy and defensive about his amputation. Implying she'd been a bad granddaughter. Showing his hurt feelings about what she'd done to him.

You'd think he was one of the at-risk kids in his own program, lashing out and blaming others.

He guessed he had the right to blame Gabby, since she'd lied about her feelings and cheated on him in a very public way. But he'd thought he'd overcome that, what with all that had happened since then.

Nope. Seeing her had brought out every immature desire to retaliate that he'd had when he'd first seen his cousin's social media post, arm slung around Gabby. "My new girl," it had said.

In his grim barracks in Afghanistan, Reese had ripped down his photo of her, discarded the letter he'd been writing, blocked her on everything.

He didn't need to go back to that time when his hope had overcome his good sense. He needed to focus on the Rescue Haven program and forget about his old dreams of love and family.

"I'm here," called a strident voice out in the barn. "Just in time for the little rebels. Want me to feed and water them?"

He went to the door. "Hey, Tammy," he said to the woman who occasionally filled in for his assistant. "Thanks for coming in on short notice. Why don't you let them hang around and see to the dogs for half an hour and then settle them down with a snack? This interview I'm doing shouldn't take long." Gabby's grand-mother had been mysterious about this candidate but had insisted the person had stellar qualifications.

An uneasy possibility occurred to him. Nana wouldn't have… No. She wouldn't be that insensitive.

Or maybe she would, because walking through the barn door was none other than Gabby herself.

He couldn't school his face in time. All the hurt, anger and disbelief must have shown, right along with the intense attraction he still felt.

She stopped walking toward him as if repelled by his powerful emotions.

He didn't need Tammy to see this interaction and spread it all over town. "My office is in here," he said gruffly. He turned and walked inside, almost hoping she wouldn't come along.

Only when he sat down behind his big, messy metal desk did he see that Gabby had followed him, but she stood in the doorway as if she wasn't sure she dared to enter. "Nana didn't tell you it was me, did she." It wasn't a question but a statement.

He shook his head, straightening papers on his desk as he tried to compose himself.

Nana had set him up, telling him she had the per-fect candidate to fill the job he so desperately needed to fill.

But Gabby had known whom she'd be working for, obviously. "Why'd you come?" he asked her. "I wouldn't think you'd want to work for me."

She was still standing in the doorway, gripping the edge of the frame, eyes wide and vulnerable. "Um, I really need a job while I'm in town. Nana said you were hiring and wanted to talk to me. Obviously, she was wrong. I'll go."

She half turned, and only then did he realize she'd dressed up; beneath her heavy parka, she was wearing nice blue pants and a white shirt, boots with a little heel. Her normally wild hair was tamed back into a bun.

She wanted the job. She was trying.

Since she'd made an effort, he should at least talk to her. A courtesy interview. It would be good for him, get him used to the fact that Gabby might be around for a few weeks. "Wait a minute," he said, and pulled out a chair for her. "Have a seat. We might as well see this through for Nana's sake."

She looked at him for a moment, shook her head. "Don't patronize me," she said, her voice low. "If you aren't going to consider me, I'll leave."

He didn't answer that because he didn't know how. "The kids are a handful," he said instead. "I need someone to work with them."

"You know I was working on a degree in education before…" She trailed off.

Before what? he wondered, but didn't ask. He'd admired her interest in teaching, her determination to get a college degree; it was part of why he hadn't pushed to get married or even engaged right after high school. He'd known that was the right thing to do when she'd been so happy about her studies the summer after her freshman year, during the friendly get-togethers that they'd kept nonromantic by mutual agreement.

After her sophomore year, when he'd been getting ready to go overseas, he'd had more trouble holding his feelings in check. He'd asked her for a commitment and she'd agreed.

And then he'd left, and everything had changed.

Shouts, barks and the sounds of a scuffle came from the barn. "Reese!" Tammy called. "Help!"

Reese was up and jogging past Gabby before Tammy finished speaking. "Be right back," he called over his shoulder.

In the middle of the barn, two of his more complicated charges were squared off and circling, both faces twisted in anger. The problem was, David was tiny, and Wolf, as he liked to be called, was huge. Between them sat a Doberman, looking back and forth while they shouted at each other.

"I can't handle these kids," Tammy said. "If nobody has raised them right…"

And that was exactly why he didn't want to hire Tammy in a permanent capacity. She had such a negative attitude toward the kids.

He waded in, putting a hand on Wolf's shoulder because he was the big one, holding up his other arm to keep David back.

"Get that thing away from me!" David reared back from Reese's hook-hand prosthetic.

Reese couldn't help the flush that came up his face. He was getting used to the amputation, a little bit, but to a kid it had to be pretty horrific.

"Dude, he's, like, a war hero, shut up!" one of the other boys said, and that made Reese flush even more.

"Yeah!"

"What's wrong with you—aren't you an American?"

More boys chimed in and a couple of them advanced on David. This was why Reese needed an assistant; Wolf was straining toward David now, too, and it took most of Reese's strength to hold him back.

Tammy stood, back pressed against the side of the barn, arms crossed protectively over herself. No help there.

"Okay, everyone." Gabby's brisk, matter-of-fact tone stopped the boys whose arms were raised to attack David. "Pretty sure Reese is going to give you some hard homework if you get into a fight. Break it up."

She was five-two and couldn't have weighed much more than one hundred pounds, but she had calm authority in her voice, and she walked right in between David and the other boys.

Even Wolf stopped pushing at Reese and tilted his head to one side, watching her.

"Anybody willing to give me a tour of the facilities?" she asked. "I'd like to see the dogs."

There was a moment's silence. Gabby maintained eye contact with first one boy, then another, until she'd worked her way around the hostile circle without saying another word.

All of a sudden, several of the boys volunteered to show her around, and the rest of them trooped along, leaving Reese free to settle Wolf on one side of the barn and David on the other. He found out what the dispute had been about and gave them both chores.

Then he watched morosely as Gabby talked and laughed with the boys, seeming completely comfortable as she knelt to look at each dog, asked questions and really listened to the answers.

Tammy pulled herself together and set out breakfast rolls, fruit and juice at the long table at one end of the barn, and that drew all of the boys to focus. She turned on the inspirational podcast they always listened to as they ate, and Reese gestured Gabby back into his office.

It didn't seem right to be angry about what she'd done, now that his cousin was gone. It was just that seeing her had brought back all the memories of what he'd hoped for, back when he'd been young and naive, thinking the world was basically a good place and that things would get better once he was grown up and free from his aunt and uncle's house.

"Nice kids," she said, her hand on the back of the chair in front of his desk. "But I assume you don't want me to work for you."

"You were good with the boys," he said.

"I like kids." She shrugged. "Plus, I get what it's like to be the one who gets in trouble."

"I'm sure you do." When Gabby had arrived in Bethlehem Springs in the fifth grade, the word was that she'd gotten sent to the principal's office most days.

She'd settled down by the time he'd arrived in middle school. He'd acted out some, too—you could hardly help it when you'd lost your parents suddenly and moved into a new school and a family who didn't much want you.

That was why he'd latched on to the job with this grant-funded program as soon as he'd been cleared to work. He felt like he understood boys who were struggling. The fact that the grant funding was running out was currently his biggest worry. "Listen," he said, "it's probably not a good idea long term, but I need help pulling this Christmas Camp together. Starting next week, all the boys will be here full days, and like you just saw, I can't handle them alone. If you're willing, I'd like to offer you a temporary contract, through Christmas."

"Really?" She stared at him. "You can work with me?"

It might kill him, but for the sake of the boys, he

could do it. "Think about it," he said. "I know you have to watch out for your grandmother. If you need to run over here and there, it's fine."

She bit her lip, opened her mouth and then closed it again.

"If you could decide in the next day or two, that would be great."

She shook her head rapidly. "I don't need a day or two. I already know I want the job."

"Then I'll draw up a contract."

"Reese…"

He looked up from his desk. "Yeah?"

"You're sure about this?"

"I'm sure. You can start on Monday."

"Okay, then." She reached across the desk, offering a handshake.

He'd already encountered that awkward move before, so he knew how to deflect it by extending his left hand. He gripped hers, and the sensation of touching her travelled straight to his heart.

She must have felt it, too, because she pulled her hand away, thanked him and hurried out of his office.

Leaving him to remember that it had always been like that with them: electric, dangerous as an exposed wire.

Now it felt more dangerous than ever.

Chapter Two

Gabby had always loved the fact that, despite being a small town, Bethlehem Springs had a train station. As a kid, she'd come here with her grandfather to watch the trains. As a restless adolescent, hanging around the station had given her a sense of being able to leave at a moment's notice, to get to the bright lights of Chicago or New York or, more realistically, Cleveland or Columbus. She'd gone to and from college on the train. And when everything had blown up in Bethlehem Springs that horrible summer after her sophomore year, she'd packed her things and taken the train to start a new life.

Today, though, she wasn't leaving; she was staying, getting more tied down and domesticated. It had been eighteen months since she'd seen her half brother at her mother's funeral, and they hadn't exactly gotten along. He'd been understandably grief stricken about losing their mother and upset at the prospect of going to live with his father, and he'd begged Gabby to let him come live with her.

But at twenty-one and pregnant with a baby she'd

in no way planned for, she hadn't felt qualified to become the guardian of a brother she barely knew. Besides, surely Jacob's father would do a better job taking care of him.

The father, unfortunately, hadn't supervised Jacob well. Her brother had gotten into trouble for some minor vandalism, and rather than help him work through it, his father had shipped the poor kid off to military school. Jacob had just completed his first term, and somehow, he was coming to spend the Christmas break with Nana rather than going back to California to stay with his father. He was to arrive on the 6:00 a.m. train.

The platform was spooky-dark, with mist rising from the ground and clouds ominous overhead. Huddled in her heavy parka on the outdoor platform, she wished she'd thought to bring mittens and a hat.

Maybe she should've borrowed a dog from Reese's kennels, too, because it was awfully creepy here. Lots of rustling in the bushes that lined the far edge of the platform. Loud, screeching noises of what might have been an owl on the hunt.

Another car arrived at the parking lot beside the platform. A man, solo, got out.

Chills shook Gabby's already shivering body. It was still black darkness outside, and according to her app, the train wouldn't arrive for another twenty minutes. Running late, like so many passenger trains did these days.

The man sat down on a bench at the other end of the platform. That was weird, right? If he'd been a normal person, he'd have come over here and said hello.

But maybe he just wasn't sociable. He carried no

luggage that she could see, so he must be picking someone up. Maybe he just treasured his last minutes of solitude.

He was looking in her direction.

Maybe he was a criminal who was going to cut her into a million pieces and throw her onto the train tracks.

"Gabby?"

Relief made her limbs go limp. It was Reese, and he was walking toward her.

"What are you doing here?" She stood to greet him, her heart still pounding just as hard as when she'd thought he was a dangerous stranger.

"I'm here to pick up a boy who's starting our program. His mom works the night shift and won't be off for another hour, so I offered to pick him up for her."

Above and beyond. That didn't surprise her; Reese had always gone the extra mile without thinking of his own convenience. "I'm here for my brother," she told him, even though he hadn't asked. But talking seemed to calm her nerves, at least a little. "He's staying with me and Nana and…me and Nana. For the holidays." She should have just casually mentioned Izzy—*Oh, didn't you know I have a baby?*—but she didn't, even though this would be Izzy's first Christmas, and Gabby hoped to make it special. Keeping Izzy's existence a secret from Reese was a cowardly thing, and fruitless— he'd find out soon enough—but she was pretty sure it would upset him, and at 6:00 a.m., she couldn't handle that. "I thought there'd be coffee here. Didn't the station used to be open, with a little concession area?"

"Hard times." He nodded at the steaming cup he was carrying. "I'd offer you some of mine, but…"

He didn't have to say it. There had been a time when sharing a beverage would have been as normal as breathing, but that time was past. "It's okay," she said. "Good for me. I'm too addicted."

"Where's your brother coming from?" He frowned down at her. "Did I even know you had a brother?"

"Probably not," she said. "He's my half brother, and I didn't really know him, didn't talk about him much. He grew up with Mom." She was over her resentment about that, mostly. Mom had raised her son—well, she'd done the best she could—but she'd dumped her daughter on Nana without a backward glance. "He's been at Smith Military Academy since September."

"That's where the kid I'm picking up—" he gestured toward the tracks "—that's where he's coming from, too."

A whistle, high and mournful, blew their way on a gust of cold wind, and then a light appeared way down the track. A moment later the train's engine was audible. Both Reese and Gabby stood.

Dawn was just lightening the edge of the sky when two boys disembarked from the train, the only passengers to do so. As they put down their duffels, stretched and looked around, the train pulled away again.

"Hey, Mr. Markowski!" The blond boy stuck out a hand in polite greeting.

"Connor. Hope you had a good trip. This is Gabby Hanks."

"Hi," Gabby said with a quick smile for the boy, but she was distracted with staring at her brother. He'd shot up several inches since she'd last seen him, and young as he was, it looked like he needed a shave.

Dark circles beneath his eyes and a pallor to his skin made him look less than healthy.

Maybe it was just that it was early. Teens didn't do well with early.

She opened her arms and pulled him into a hug. "It's good to see you, Jacob."

He didn't hug her back, but he submitted to her affection, probably the best you could expect from a fifteen-year-old boy.

They all turned and walked toward the parking lot. Each of the boys carried a small duffel bag, and they wore khakis and heavy wool jackets, identical. Must have been some kind of civilian uniform from the military academy.

"So you two know each other?" Reese asked, clearly trying to make conversation.

"Yeah. Some. He's a year ahead of me." Connor looked more than a year younger than Jacob, but then, kids developed at such different rates.

As Gabby walked along, half beside and half behind her silent brother, the reality of what the next few weeks would be like started to settle in.

Nana was sick. She was insistent that she could take care of Izzy, but even if that turned out to be the case, she wouldn't have much energy left to entertain Jacob. Gabby herself would be busy working full-time. And anyway, a fifteen-year-old boy didn't want to hang out with his grandmother and his older half sister whom he barely knew.

The wireless connection in Nana's house was spotty at best, so the internet as entertainment couldn't be counted on.

Watching Reese talk easily with the other boy,

Gabby got a brainstorm, the obvious solution. "Go ahead and get in the car," she said to Jacob, tossing him the keys. "I'm going to talk to Reese for a minute."

She caught Reese's eye and beckoned him over. "What's the age range for boys in your kids' program?" she asked.

"We don't have an official limit, but I think our youngest is eleven and our oldest, let's see, he's fifteen." He clicked open his car for Connor. "Why do you ask?"

"How do kids get into the program? Could Jacob participate?"

"There's paperwork to be done," he said, frowning. "It's based on financial need."

"Pretty sure he has that. He's on scholarship at school, I know."

Reese's brow wrinkled, and he started to shake his head. He was going to say no.

"Please, Reese? It's just for the Christmas break." She lowered her voice. "He'll go nuts with boredom at Nana's, and that wouldn't be good for a kid with his history."

Reese looked thoughtfully toward Gabby's car, where Jacob was fiddling with the radio. His face softened. "I know what that's like. I'll see what I can do."

"Thank you." She shot Reese a grateful smile and then hurried over to the passenger side of her car and opened the door. "Jacob, come out and talk to Reese a minute. He's involved with a program that might be really good for you over this break."

Jacob didn't look particularly thrilled, but he dutifully came out of the car, walked around to where

Reese was standing, wiped his hand on his jeans and held it out to shake.

Gabby did the introductions. "Reese Markowski, I'd like to present Jacob Hanks, my brother."

"Pleased to meet you," Reese said.

But Jacob's lip curled and he pulled back his hand. "Markowski? As in, the Markowskis who live on Elder Lane?"

Reese nodded. "That's my aunt and uncle. Do you know them?"

"Oh, I know them," Jacob said. "I know them well enough to know that I don't want anything to do with them, or any program they're connected with."

"Jacob! Be polite!" Gabby knew the Markowskis could be hard to deal with, but she didn't want Jacob to ruin his chances to do something constructive with his break. "I didn't know you'd ever spent enough time here to meet Reese's aunt and uncle."

"Last summer," he growled, and then Gabby remembered. She'd been so overwhelmed over on the other side of the state, what with working and caring for Izzy, that she'd barely registered the fact that Jacob had visited Nana last summer. Now that she thought about it, Nana had told her the visit was going on a bit longer than scheduled.

Reese's eyes narrowed. "What happened?"

"I don't want to go into it." Jacob dug his hands deeper into his pockets and stared at the ground.

Reese watched him, and compassion crossed his face. "My aunt and uncle can be difficult," he said. "If it makes you feel any better, I was the outcast kid in that family. The poor cousin who came to live with them after my parents died. So I'm not exactly one of them."

Jacob's eyes flashed toward Reese's face for a second of raw connection. Gabby guessed he hadn't met many people who had lost their parents young. She knew herself that it made her feel different from others her age. How much more that must be the case for a teenager.

Reese had always seemed a little sad, a little haunted. It had given him strength and understanding beyond the other high school boys; that had been a part of his appeal. She could see that he still had that going for him, just from the kind way he spoke to her half brother.

"It would be something for you to do over the break," Gabby said. "Why don't you give it a chance?"

"I'd like to have you join us," Reese said. "I could use another older boy. Role models for the younger ones."

"Are you kidding me? You think I might be a role model?" Jacob rolled his eyes at Gabby. "Talk to your aunt and uncle, is all I can say."

"I will. But a lot of the kids in the program have issues. The past is the past."

Gratitude washed over Gabby. Reese was really trying to make this work, just on the strength of her and Jacob's and Nana's needs.

"I don't want to do it." Jacob shrugged and blew out a breath, making his long bangs puff up, and suddenly, despite the beard stubble, he looked like a little kid. "All I want to do is take a nap. Do we have to decide about this right now?"

Reese chuckled. "That's about the smartest thing anyone has said all day," he said. "Gabby, I'll see you

Monday morning. You can bring Jacob if he decides he wants to come, as long as his official guardian agrees. We can do the paperwork then."

"Thanks," Gabby said faintly. She couldn't believe that Reese had so readily agreed to take in the teenager. But she shouldn't have been surprised. That was who he was.

The problem was, seeing him be a compassionate man was making her fall for him again, even harder than she had when she was in high school. And because of what had happened, he was the last man she should get involved with.

Two days later, right after Sunday services, Reese wiped his brow in the overly heated meeting room just off the fellowship hall. The presentation to the church board and a small audience from the congregation wasn't going especially well, but it wasn't going badly.

Reese felt like he had some impressive charts and statistics, but members of the board kept looking out the window at the flurries that had started to fall. A lot of them were nervous drivers and didn't like to drive in any kind of bad weather, even in broad daylight.

Ideally, they'd agree to fund his program for the next year and hurry home to Sunday dinner. He answered a couple of questions and then looked to the chairperson, hoping to get a quick vote.

And then Santiago Romano stood, leaning on his cane, dark eyes challenging. "When you proposed this program, I didn't think it would be for *that* kind of kids," Mr. Romano said. "I was picturing more of a friendly day camp for kids whose parents have to work while they're on school break."

"That's what it is." Reese tried to keep the irritation out of his voice, because he knew exactly what Mr. Romano meant. But he wasn't going to say it himself. If the man wanted to show his snobbery, the words needed to come out of his own mouth. "The kids in the program, for the most part, have parents who are working, some of them two jobs. The Rescue Haven program has been giving them something constructive to do after school since September, and now, that support is continuing through the Christmas vacation."

"But these are kids in trouble," Mr. Romano said stubbornly. "Kids who may get into more trouble when they're all together in a gang, at loose ends all day."

"The point is, they won't *be* at loose ends if you continue to fund the program," Reese said. "They're working with dogs other people have abandoned, helping to train and rehabilitate them. And doing sports, and games, and having meals together." Reese hesitated, not wanting to call the older man out, but he needed to speak up for his boys. "Rather than calling them kids in trouble, I prefer to call them kids at risk."

"Are we a church who won't take risks?" Nana's best friend, Bernadette Williams, was the oldest member of the board, though only by a year or two. "Risks are how great things get accomplished. I like what Reese is doing. These young people need something to bring out the best in them. Reese knows about that, and he'll do a good job with it."

"Hear, hear," came a voice from the small audience. It sounded like Nana, but Reese couldn't see her.

If Nana was here, did that mean Gabby was, as well?

Reese scanned the room. Board members sat at a large conference table, and interested members of the congregation occupied several rows of chairs at the back of the room.

He hoped some of the other board members would speak up in support, but they were silent.

Reese knew why. They respected Bernadette's opinions, but Mr. Romano's money funded so many of the church's outreaches that everyone was hesitant to offend him.

Time to bring out the big guns. "I have here a copy of the church's mission," Reese said, pulling it up on his smartphone. "To spread the gospel of Jesus, through actions as much as through words, with a special mission for the poor." He looked up and focused on Bernadette's smiling face. "That's exactly what I'm trying to do. I'd like to respectfully request continuation of funding for the next calendar year."

Mr. Romano must have heard the murmurs of approval throughout the room, because he switched tactics. "I wasn't expecting the program to be right next door to me," he said. "You have those kids on the edge of town, close to some of our bigger homes, where stealing is a big temptation. Don't they pose a danger to the community?"

"They're well supervised, and we haven't had any problems with the after-school program." Thus far, the kids had limited their bad behavior to arguing with each other. Well, and nearly coming to blows, but there was no need to mention that. "As for the property, I did a lot of due diligence," Reese went on. "I leased the best property I could find, for the best price. I want to be a good steward of the donors' resources."

"Yeah, well, that property has always been an eyesore." Mr. Romano's grumble was quiet, but Reese heard it and winced inwardly. He hated to see the old man reduced to insults.

"Permission to speak?" The clear voice from the audience belonged to Nana. So she *was* here. There was some shifting around as Gabby helped her to stand and walk out to a small podium set up in the aisle between the rows of chairs.

Reese's heart gave a great thump. He hadn't seen Gabby at church, and now the sight of her in a green sweater, denim skirt and high boots went directly to his heart.

Reese's neck heated. He wanted to impress her—still, which was ridiculous—and he wasn't looking exactly stellar right now.

Not that that mattered. Not at all. He wasn't trying to build a relationship with Gabby; it would never work, and besides that, he wasn't even interested. She'd dumped him before and she'd do it again.

"I believe there's something in the Bible that talks about not building up mansions on earth," Nana said. "If I don't want to spend money making my house a showpiece, I have my reasons for it. I donate to the church's outreach programs. And while I can't donate as much cash as some—" she eyed Santiago Romano "—I do what I can. Including giving this program an excellent deal on rental of the barn and fields."

"There's no Bible verse about not building mansions, Estelle," Mr. Romano said, a smile in his voice.

"I can quote it." Nana glared at him. "'Lay not up for yourselves treasures upon earth, where moth and rust doth corrupt, and where thieves break through and steal.' Matthew six, verses nineteen and twenty."

"There's more to that passage," Mr. Romano sputtered.

"Yes, there is." Nana was still standing, and now she pointed a bony finger at Mr. Romano. "It has to do with laying up treasures in heaven, which is what this young man—" she nodded at Reese "—is trying to do."

Mr. Romano still looked ready to argue. He opened his mouth.

"And what's more," Nana said, cutting him off, "it is easier for a camel to go through the eye of a needle than for a rich man to enter the kingdom of God. That's in the book of Matthew, sir, said by our Lord Himself. Even you can't argue with Jesus."

Reese could barely stifle a laugh at how thoroughly Nana had shut down Mr. Romano.

Gabby put an arm around Nana and encouraged her back into her seat as murmurs went through the crowd. Some were amused, because the feud between Mr. Romano and Nana went back years. Some sounded more disapproving; a board member behind Reese was speaking, and Reese overheard the words *inappropriate* and *not the right place*.

Bernadette cleared her throat and stood, and the room quieted down. "I do have a concern, Reese," she said. "Do you have enough help to run this Christmas-break program, given that your main assistant had to leave unexpectedly?"

"I'm in the process of hiring a new assistant," Reese said.

"Tammy?" Bernadette's voice held the faintest tinge of skepticism. Around the room, people were looking at one another, and Reese knew why. Tammy's heart was in the right place, but she didn't have a reputation for being focused and responsible.

"No," Reese said before the murmurs could rise louder. "The candidate I'm working with has most of a degree in education and a lot of good ideas."

"May I ask who it is? Someone from Bethlehem Springs?" Bernadette was still standing.

While Reese was glad she had taken charge of the discussion, getting Mr. Romano off center stage, he knew how insistent Bernadette could be when it was a question of doing the right thing. "It's Gabby Hanks," he said.

A murmur rose in the room. Reese looked around, wondering what it was about.

But Bernadette gave a nod, put her hands on her hips and looked around the room until the murmuring stopped. "I suggest we see what Reese can do. If he manages the children well through this break, then we'll know the program can be expanded, and we'll have a better basis to fund it through the next year."

"But how will we know if he manages it well?" the board's accountant, Mike Watson, asked. "What criteria are we using? How will we assess the outcomes?"

Bernadette opened her mouth to speak, but there was another flurry back in Nana's part of the room, and then Gabby stood. Her cheeks were pink, her mouth determined. "How about if we have the kids and animals do some kind of a performance for the church? A Christmas performance?"

"What's your vision, Gabby?" Bernadette asked. "How would that help us assess the results?"

Reese didn't know how he'd lost control of this discussion, but he needed to take it back. He opened his mouth to speak.

Gabby gave him a look, and because of their history together, he read it instantly. *I've got this, relax*, she seemed to say with her eyes. "If the boys are able to work together toward a productive goal that entertains the community, that'll show that they can work toward other productive goals," she said. "And by attending and supporting the performance, the church members can show that they understand our mission." She looked pointedly at Santiago Romano as she said it.

Reese hid a small smile. Despite the fact that this was likely to be a disaster, he admired Gabby's spunk.

Gabby glanced at Reese, then went on. "The Sunday before Christmas, or the early Christmas Eve service, might be good times to give the pastor and choirs a break. But we could do it on a weeknight instead. Whatever would help out the church."

Mr. Romano started to laugh. "Boy, if you can pull that off with those kids, you'll be doing something very surprising."

"Christmas *is* the season of wonderful surprises," Gabby said gently.

"That it is," Bernadette said. "If we can all agree to this proposal, we can get on the road and home to our families. I'd suggest Tuesday evening, the twenty-third, which gives you just over a week. All in favor?"

Thank you, Bernadette. Everyone wanted to get home. There was a chorus of ayes, and just a couple of nays, one belonging to Mr. Romano. No surprise there.

As people hurried to gather their coats and hats, Reese blew out a breath. Thanks to Gabby, he now had a clear-cut goal. With a breathtakingly short time line.

He had to make this program a success. With his disability, he couldn't do what he'd always planned to do, carpentry. And he seriously doubted that he could form a family; even before he'd become disabled, he'd never been especially smooth with women. The one woman he'd fallen in love with—Gabby— had dumped him.

If he could make a go of this program, he could have a different kind of a family, and meaning in his life.

Few people gathered around the coffeepot afterward, but Gabby was among them, and he tapped her on the shoulder and gestured her off to the side. "You've set us up to do something difficult," he said.

"I'm sorry. It just came to me."

She looked so penitent that he felt bad. "I'm not upset about it. It's a good idea," he said, and when her face brightened, his heart lifted, too. He needed to get himself under control. They were working together and that was it. "It's definitely going to be a challenge, and we need to get started right away. Can you meet me this afternoon so we can start to figure out how we're going to make it work?"

She glanced at Nana, still seated. "I think I can," she said.

That made Reese realize that he hadn't seen young Jacob at the church service. He wondered how things were going in the household.

Still, it was Gabby who had brought up this possibility, and Reese knew next to nothing about putting on a show. "I really need you to step up and help with it," he said.

She nodded. "I'll do my best," she said, her voice subdued.

So now, rather than his usual quiet Sunday afternoon avoiding his aunt and uncle's family gathering, Reese was going to be working with the very pretty lady who'd already broken his heart once.

He just had to make sure he didn't let her do it again.

Chapter Three

"I'm so glad Cleo's Crafts and Café is still here." Gabby sipped peppermint hot chocolate and looked around the cozy place. Steam blurred the windows, making the café its own little world. There were only about ten tables. Up front, a pastry case held Cleo's famous concoctions, heavily leaning toward Christmas items at this time of year: chocolate pinwheel cookies and gingerbread boys and chocolate-pecan chess pie.

Reese looked around, too. "You haven't been gone that long, have you?" He sipped his own flavored coffee. "I'm surprised you're surprised."

"It seems like forever ago." Then she flushed, because she wasn't referring to the last time she'd been home; she was referring to their high school years, when they'd been falling in love.

"It's different because we're different," he said. Maybe he didn't know it, but his hand went to his arm. Today, he was wearing a prosthetic, obvious because of the pincerlike hook in place of his right hand.

Curiosity won out over decorum. "Why do you wear a prosthetic some days and not others?"

"Getting used to it. It's a process." He leveled a steady gaze at her. "*You* seem different from when we were kids, too."

I'm different because I'm a mom. "We should figure out the show," she said briskly, trying to get back to business. And avoid telling him about Izzy. Which shouldn't be a big deal, but she hated the thought of his questions. Despite all her counseling, she still felt a heated rush of shame at the idea of talking about it. "I feel bad to have volunteered you for something you don't want to do, but I think it'll be great."

"Maybe." He shrugged. "Tell me what you were thinking. I don't exactly have a vision."

She pulled out a pad of paper and a pen. "Tell me about your boys. Ages, abilities, things like that."

He nodded, sipping coffee. "Like I mentioned to Jacob, they're eleven to fifteen. But skewed toward the younger side. I think we have…three each of eleven- and twelve-year-olds. Two thirteen-year-olds, and one each of fourteen and fifteen. Two fifteen-year-olds if Jacob joins."

She nodded, making notes. "And how do the dogs fit in?" She'd seen them when she'd been in the barn before: the one Doberman that seemed to roam around, a row of kennels in the back of the barn and an open yard area separate from where the boys gathered in the front.

"In a way, the dogs are similar to the boys," he said wryly. "Most have behavior problems and that's why they were surrendered."

"All breeds?"

He nodded. "But I try to make it so there's one dog per boy. Their job is to train that one dog."

She put down her pen. "Uh-oh. Will Jacob mess that up? Can he get a dog this late in the game?"

"There are always dogs that need help," he said. "See, the overall vision is…" He trailed off, looking just a little shy.

"Tell me." She set her cup down and leaned forward a little. Reese had always been a dreamer, the rare kind who could put his dreams into action. When she'd been falling in love with him in high school, his dreams had been of beautiful cabinets and chairs and tables he could make. He'd looked at a piece of wood, even scrap wood, and seen all its possibilities.

"Well. I got into training dogs, a little, in rehab." He made a disparaging gesture toward his prosthetic. "They had therapy dogs, and I kind of bonded with one of them who was about to flunk out. Got him over his fear of prosthetics, actually. Showed a talent, so they gave me a couple other troubled dogs to train."

"That's cool, but how'd you learn to do it? I mean, your aunt and uncle had Fifi, but…"

He rolled his eyes. "Fifi. May she rest in peace after eighteen years of giving everyone nothing but trouble."

"She wasn't exactly trained, it's true." Gabby chuckled. "She did have a lot of cute outfits, though."

"Don't remind me. But you know…" He trailed off, looking thoughtful. "I'd guess that, now, with what I've learned, I could actually train Fifi."

She was fascinated, because he'd taken on the same dreamy-yet-passionate look he'd had when she'd known him years ago. "How did you learn what you know?"

"Online videos. Books. After I got better, they let me take a couple of dogs through agility training."

"All this was through the VA?"

He nodded. "Because while I thought I was reha-bilitating dogs, I was actually getting rehabilitated my-self." He sipped coffee. "So when I came home, and there was no possibility of carpentry, there was a need for someone to take over a grant-funded after-school program for at-risk boys. I added the element of dog training, and…Rescue Haven was born."

"I have a feeling there was more to it." But she admired his sense of industry, going directly into another line of work. "Reese, can I ask…why'd you come back to Bethlehem Springs?"

He looked out the window. The street was busy with people: couples strolling, families with kids, Christ-mas shoppers overloaded with bags. "My aunt and uncle needed me."

"But they always—" She broke off. "I'm impressed that you did that for them, is all."

"Because they favored Brock? Didn't really want to take me in? I know," he said. "But when he passed, they were devastated. Aunt Catherine, especially. My uncle came to visit me at the VA hospital and asked me to come back for at least a year, just to try to pull her out of her slump."

She stared at him, remembering the cold, snobbish woman who'd rarely had a kind word for anyone. "You did that for her."

He shrugged. "Uncle Clive pulled strings to get me funding for the dog aspect of the Rescue Haven pro-gram," he explained. "I figured, if I couldn't do what I wanted to do, at least I could do some good." He drained his coffee. "Come on. Let's walk and talk."

She remembered that about him, then, that he always preferred to be moving. It was why he'd wanted to work with his hands rather than in an office; it was part of the reason he'd gone into the military.

They carried their cups to the counter and then headed outside.

The sun peeked through clouds, and there was a dusting of snow on the ground. The cold air made Gabby wrap her scarf around her neck and put up her furry hood. Reese, just like he used to, went bare-headed.

The temptation to reach for his hand was strong. They'd flowed so easily back into talking, just like old times. Sharing dreams.

He looked down at her as they walked, and she got the strangest feeling that he was fighting the same impulse. They'd strolled down these streets together so many times.

But he looked away and straightened. "Anyway," he said, his voice going businesslike, "we should fig-ure out this show, because we're going to need to start practicing and getting organized right away."

"True." She frowned, thinking. "It's got to be a kids and dogs show, somehow. Ooh, let's go into Mistletoe from Mindy," she said as they turned a corner. "It's sure to give us some ideas."

"You think?" he asked, sounding skeptical. But he held the door for her while they walked into the Christmas-themed shop. The scents of pine and gingerbread filled the air, and every possible display spot held ornaments, garlands and Christmas dishes.

Gabby spun slowly, looking at everything. "We should bring the boys here. It'll help them get creative."

Reese groaned. "The thought of all those big, clumsy boys in here... No. Just no."

"Then what do you suggest?"

"It's in a church," he said. "Shouldn't it be, like, a nativity pageant or something?"

"Dressing the dogs up like stable animals?" She frowned. "That would be cute, but would the boys go for it?"

"Doubtful," he said.

She'd learned in her education classes that kids needed a sense of control. "In fact, we probably should let them do the planning, make up the show."

He stared at her. "Do you know how...*inappropriate* a bunch of boys can be?"

"Oh, I'm sure they can." She fingered a Santa ornament. "But if we explain to them that it's for a church, and that it will help keep the program going, they may step up."

He looked skeptical as they meandered through the shop.

"The alternative is having them sneer through a kid-like program they hate." She was thinking of Jacob now.

"You have a good point," he admitted. "At the same time, this is really important to me. The show is like a test. Do we really want to leave it in the hands of a small group of troubled boys?"

She bit her lip. "It's scary. But if we explain how high the stakes are..."

"Let me think about it," he said as they reached the door again and headed out of the shop. "That's going to take an awful lot of trust."

"In the boys?"

"In God," he said.

She tilted her head, looking at him. *That* wasn't something the younger Reese would have said.

"How about we ask Jacob his opinion? That'll give us a test run of what the boys might think of, and also draw him into the program." He met her eyes, his own crinkling in the now bright sunlight.

She drew in a sharp breath. Reese was so handsome. Tall, muscular and athletic, with those rare blue eyes that stood out against his dark complexion and hair.

Add a sincere faith and compassion into the mix, and he was almost irresistible.

Except she *had* to resist him. Because he was inevitably going to find out about Izzy, and she knew intuitively how much that would upset him. They'd both valued saving intimacy for marriage.

That choice had been taken away from Gabby.

Reese could never, ever find out about the circumstances of Izzy's conception. That would devastate him and his whole family. And even though she knew better intellectually, it would cause her shame.

So she needed to flip the switch on this attraction to Reese. Unfortunately, she had the feeling it wasn't going to be easy to do.

That night, Reese looked down at the big, drooling dog beside him and took a deep breath. "I don't know if this'll work, Biff. You'll have to be on good behavior."

The dog ignored him, lifting his leg in the light of the streetlamp in front of Nana's house.

So much for making a good impression. He urged

the dog up the porch steps, brushed a hand over his hair and reached down to adjust Biff's floppy ear before ringing Nana's doorbell.

Jacob opened the door, which Reese figured was a good sign. At least the teen wasn't sulking in his room.

In fact, when he looked past Jacob, he saw a puzzle on a card table in the middle of the living room. Gabby and Nana were sitting at the table, and a soda by a third chair suggested that Jacob had been working on the puzzle, too. A Christmas movie was on the old-fashioned TV in the corner. Evergreen garlands looped up the stair railing, and a small, lopsided tree stood in the corner, half-decorated.

The house was shabby, but Reese had always appreciated how homey it was.

"I was hoping I could come in and talk to you for a few minutes," he said to Jacob. "Problem is, I have someone with me. Would your grandmother mind if I brought in a dog?"

Jacob looked down, and his eyes widened. "Come on in," he said, and pulled the door wide open.

"Sit," Reese commanded, keeping the dog in the entryway.

Biff cocked his enormous head as if he was trying to understand.

Reese gave up and looked past Jacob to Nana. "Biff is big, but gentle," he said. "I was hoping to talk to Jacob for a few minutes about him, but I know not everyone likes dogs in the house. Should I take him back outside?"

"Come in, come in," she said in her raspy voice. "We'd love to have a visit. Gabby, could you take his coat and get him something to drink?"

"Um, sure." There was a pause, and then Gabby stood. She seemed to swallow before walking across the room and then holding out a hand for his coat. Her smile looked forced, and it seemed as if she was dragging her feet with every step. She didn't even seem to notice the dog.

Reese must have misread her signals this afternoon. He had gotten the feeling that maybe Gabby still had some of the old feelings. But now she looked like she'd rather see anyone else than him.

Focus on the boy and dog, he counseled himself.

"Can I get you something to drink?" Her words were wooden.

"No. I won't be staying long." *Since you're obviously not happy to see me.* "I just wanted to get a little input from Jacob before we talk to the rest of the boys about the show tomorrow. And introduce him to Biff."

Jacob was standing a few feet away from the dog, staring at him. "Why do you want to introduce me to this dog?"

"Because I'm hoping you'll take him on as your project," he said, "if you decide to do our program. He's a little much for the other boys to handle, but since you're bigger and older than most of them, I think you'd be good at it. Up to you, though."

Gabby gave him a quick glance, looking much more friendly. *Thank you*, she mouthed to him.

Warmth suffused his chest. He was glad he'd come.

"I don't know much about dogs," Jacob said, "but I'd like to learn."

Now Gabby and Nana stared at each other, eyebrows raised in identical expressions. Reese was guessing that Jacob's attitude hadn't been consistently upbeat and eager to learn thus far.

"Terrific." Reese kept his voice casual. You didn't want to show too much enthusiasm around teenagers or they'd balk. "Maybe you could get to know him a little. And would you mind talking to Gabby and me about this show we're being asked to put on?"

"Sure."

They walked into the front room, and Gabby turned down the sound on the television. Quickly, Reese explained about the show and how important it was. "So we were thinking the boys could plan the show, but I'm wondering whether they'll be up to it. Wanted to get a teenager's perspective."

"We watch videos all the time," Jacob said with a shrug. "Probably could make a show like some of those."

"Those music videos are full of bad language," Nana said. "Why, I've learned words I never heard in my life, volunteering down at the mission for families."

"The show's going to be in a church. There can't be any bad language." Gabby looked at Jacob. "Do you think the boys will be able to do that?"

"How would I know?" Jacob stuffed his hands into his pockets, still staring at the dog. "I don't even know these kids."

Reese accepted Jacob's mood shift with equanimity. He'd learned a ton about kids in a few short months, and that went with the territory. "What would make a project like that fun for you?"

"Being able to do whatever we wanted," Jacob said. "And music."

"Like Christmas carols?" Gabby asked.

"No way!" Jacob said. "But…"

"Yeah?" Reese dangled a treat in front of Biff's nose, trying to get him to lie down. It didn't work.

"There is some good Christmas music that's popular," Jacob said reluctantly. "Maybe the guys would go for that."

"Maybe you could help talk them into it." Reese kept his eyes on the dog, not wanting to pressure Jacob too much. "You're older and from out of town. They might listen to you."

"That's if I do the program."

"Right." Reese stood to leave. "I sure hope you do, for Biff's sake, if nothing else." He pounded the dog's side. "He doesn't seem to be learning anything I try to teach him."

Jacob reached out a hand and touched Biff's head, and his face morphed into a smile as he ran a hand over the dog's soft ears.

A sound came from one of the bedrooms at the back of the house. It sounded almost like… Yes, that was a baby's cry, now rising to a higher volume.

Huh? Reese looked at the three people gathered. "You have a baby here?"

Nana smiled. "My great-granddaughter," she said proudly.

"Who never shuts up," Jacob added, rolling his eyes.

Gabby looked sick.

Reese tried to puzzle this out. Nana's great-granddaughter must be… He stared at Gabby.

"I was hoping she was down for the night," Nana said. "Guess that's too much to ask for from a nine-month-old baby."

Reese's head was spinning. "Whose baby?" he asked as he did the math in his mind.

The baby's cries got louder.

"Better go get her," Nana said to Gabby, who'd been standing as if paralyzed, looking toward the back of the house.

Without a glance at Reese, Gabby left the room.

Nana watched after her proudly. "She's such a good mom. Hasn't had an easy time of it, but she does a fine job."

He knelt to pet the dog, counting the months again, hoping he was wrong.

He wasn't. Anger surged inside him.

Gabby's baby must have been conceived the summer he'd left for the Middle East. Early in the summer, if she was nine months old now.

But they'd been together early in the summer. He'd left at the end of June.

That meant her baby had been conceived while they were dating. And he knew 100 percent that he wasn't the father. He'd respected her boundaries, shared them. They'd never gone beyond a kiss.

Apparently, she hadn't kept the same boundaries with someone else…even while she was promising Reese that she cared and would wait for him.

Chapter Four

Gabby had hoped that Reese would have settled down by Monday morning, but as soon as she pushed open the barn door and saw his face—narrow eyes, clenched jaw—she knew it hadn't happened.

Most of the boys had already arrived, and she checked the time on her phone. 9:00 a.m., but apparently she and Jacob should arrive earlier, quarter till at the latest.

She put her purse and the file folder of ideas she'd brought onto the shelf outside of Reese's office, amid the sound of boys yelling and laughing, quiet country music playing and dogs barking. Bales of hay and heaps of straw sent their fragrance through the air.

It could have been kind of idyllic. But there was Jacob, already off in a corner and standing sullenly by himself. There were two of the boys clearly trying to impress the others by baiting one of the dogs, holding a toy in front of its nose and then jerking it away. And when she started toward them to put a stop to it, there was Reese, stepping in front of her, giving her a dismissive wave that clearly said he didn't think she was competent to take care of the situation.

Meeting their deadline, putting a show together in a week, wasn't going to be easy. Especially if Reese was hating on her.

Without consulting her or acting like she was a part of things, Reese called the boys together and explained the need for a show. He suggested that they look on-line for some Christmas pageant scripts, which didn't exactly make the boys enthusiastic. She waited for him to mention the idea of letting the boys take some control and making up their own show, but he didn't.

He was discounting her ideas and keeping her out of the authority loop, making her seem like just a helper. It wasn't the way he'd described the job to her, but she needed to make money, and she needed for this job to work. It was best for Jacob, for Nana and for Izzy.

She should just hold back, let him run the program the way he wanted to run it, stay on the sidelines. But when a couple of boys started covertly punching each other while Reese was trying unsuccessfully to get Jacob to share his ideas, she couldn't keep quiet.

Maybe letting the boys have a strong voice in planning their own show would be a disaster, but would it be any worse than what was happening right now? She raised her hand, and when Reese didn't notice, she stood and waved her hand more visibly, at the same time stepping between the two boys who were fighting.

"Could I make a suggestion?" she asked. "And I'd need everyone to pay attention," she added, looking sternly at the boys who'd been fighting.

Oh, how Reese wanted to say no: it was obvious,

written in every tense line of his body. But to his credit, he didn't display his lack of enthusiasm in front of the kids. "Go ahead," he said.

"Maybe some of the boys could brainstorm about an original show while others do online research about Christmas pageants that are already out there. We could regroup and report out. I think that would help some of the boys focus." She gave another warning glance to the two fighting boys, to let them know she was onto their tricks. "And if you don't have a different idea for grouping them, I'm going to suggest that we count off."

Reese frowned. "How about the boys can choose whether they want to work on original ideas or do research. Original-idea guys, over at the table. Research guys, gather around the computers. And anyone who doesn't choose, we'll count you off and assign you to a group."

The boys immediately went to one group or the other, probably because nobody wanted to get counted off like kindergartners. The group around original ideas was bigger, but there were enough boys willing to cluster around the program's two laptops that it wasn't too bad of a discrepancy. By unspoken agreement, she and Reese circulated between the two groups, and eventually, both hummed along in a rowdy kind of productivity.

She kept glancing over at Reese, but he never met her eyes. Of course not. He was furious that she'd conceived a baby while they were dating, at least, as he saw it.

The idea of talking to him about it made her insides twist. She hated thinking about that horrible night.

She'd had counseling, yes, and she'd sort of dealt with it, but she still felt that slick twist of shame every time she approached it mentally, so she usually refocused on other things whenever thoughts of Izzy's conception came up.

Avoiding the subject wasn't doable now, though. She was going to have to work with Reese, and if he was going to be sullen and angry, it would be conveyed to the boys. It would interfere with the job they had to do. That wasn't right.

When the boys showed signs of being pretty involved with their projects, she approached Reese, heart pounding. "Could we talk for a few minutes?" she asked.

He frowned. "Don't you think they need supervision?"

"Well…" She shrugged. "Yes, but I also think we need to clear the air. How about if we meet in the outer office where we can keep an eye on them?"

His lips tightened and he looked off to the side. He was going to say no.

But finally, he nodded.

She followed him to the anteroom of his office, stopping when he turned to face her. His arms were crossed, his expression set.

Her heart sank. Could she speak the truth to someone as closed-off as Reese? Someone she'd once loved, or thought she did?

Part of the truth, at least. She cleared her throat. "Last night, you found out I have a child," she began.

He looked out toward the boys. A muscle jumped in his jaw.

"I know it must have made you angry."

"I have no right to get angry," he said, still without looking at her. "It's in the past."

"I agree you have no right," she said, "but you *are* angry. And if we're going to work together, I think I need to tell you a few things."

He sighed and met her eyes. "Look, Gabby, I really don't want to talk about it."

"Don't talk, then. Listen." She drew in a breath. She couldn't tell him about his cousin. When Brock had died only hours after assaulting her, she'd made the decision not to disturb his family's memory of him. She wasn't crazy about Brock's parents, but they'd been devastated about the loss of their only son. She'd prayed about it, and talked to her counselor about it and decided not to add to their trauma.

Now, after a year and a half, no one would believe her, least of all Reese.

Brock had been a popular athlete; she was a poor girl from the wrong side of the tracks. He'd warned her not to tell anyone, asserting that they wouldn't believe she hadn't consented, right before getting drunkenly into the car that he'd driven to his death.

She didn't respect Brock's opinion about much, but she knew he was right about that.

Now, to Reese, she'd say what she could of the truth. "I could tell you were counting the months," she said, "and from your reaction, I'd guess you're thinking Izzy was conceived when we were seeing each other. But she was six weeks premature."

He looked skeptical. "Convenient excuse."

Anger fired inside her, a hot ball in her chest. "Actually, it wasn't convenient at all. She almost died, and I did, too, from preeclampsia." What she didn't say was that she'd *wanted* to die.

Most of that was about the assault and carrying Brock's baby. Lots of hormones washing around in her system. Being isolated as a pregnant girl, then a young mother in a college town full of partying teenagers.

And the fact that you'd dumped me by email didn't help.

She'd thought they had a great relationship. When she'd pulled herself back together after the assault, all she'd wanted was to talk to Reese, cry on his shoulder even if by phone. But she hadn't been able to reach him for several weeks.

She'd thought he was busy with soldier stuff, but in mid-August, she'd gotten the stiff, cold email from him: *I don't want to be involved with you anymore. Please stop contacting me.*

In the year and a half since then, she'd gained some perspective. Wartime did things to people, not the least of which was throwing soldiers together in intense, emotional situations. He'd probably met someone else, or realized he wanted to, and hadn't known how to tell her.

She'd gotten over it, or mostly. Been too busy to think about it. Moved on. Could he do the same?

His eyebrows came together as he studied her, and she could see the debate inside him of whether to believe her about Izzy's being premature.

When he didn't speak, just kept looking at her, she spread her hands and shrugged. "Look, it's nothing to do with you and I'm not going to dig up medical records to prove she was premature. I just wanted to let you know that I didn't… That nothing happened when we were dating."

"So it happened when you went back to college… Sorry." He held up a hand, shook his head. "Never mind. Not my business."

She hesitated. "Right." And then she felt like a liar. She meant he was right that it wasn't his business, but of course, Izzy hadn't been conceived back at college, but right here in Bethlehem Springs. He'd think she was agreeing with him that she'd been conceived at college.

But did it matter, when she wasn't ever going to tell him the full circumstances of what had happened?

"Is her father…involved?"

She swallowed. "No."

Sweat dripped down between her shoulder blades despite the cold day. Her stomach churned. Talking about Izzy's father with Reese felt surreal. She didn't know if she could handle much more of it. She should never have taken this job.

In fact, she felt like running away, and she even turned toward the door. But looking out, she caught a glimpse of her brother's endearing cowlick, saw him laughing with a couple of other boys.

Doing this program was going to be good for Jacob. And working this close to Nana's house would be good for both Nana and Izzy.

Gabby's own sensitive feelings didn't figure into the equation, couldn't. She stiffened her spine and turned back to Reese. "Are we all right here? Can we work together without you acting hostile toward me?"

"Of course," he said. His eyes held something like compassion. "I'm sorry I reacted in such an immature way, Gabby. I seemed to sort of plunge back into the way I felt when I found out… Well. After I was overseas. I'm more mature now, I hope, and I'll try to act it."

Curious wording. What had he found out when he'd been overseas? His brief note hadn't indicated any reason for ending things, but she'd figured he'd lost the feelings he'd had for her in their younger days.

He couldn't have found out Brock had assaulted her. No one had known about that.

Water under the bridge.

She'd always held a faint hope, in the back of her mind, that he would think about her fondly, want to reconnect. Now, she knew he'd been dealing with rehab. And she, of course, had been learning to be a mother.

They'd both been through a lot. Now he was offering to let the past go. "Thank you," she said.

"We'd better get back to the boys." He leaned to the side to scan the open barn area where they were working.

"Do you mind if I call Nana first? She was coughing a lot this morning and I want to see if she needs to visit a doctor."

"No problem. I'll handle them." He started to head out, then turned back. "Is your grandmother well enough to take care of a baby?"

Gabby bit her lip. "I worry about that myself, but whenever she's with Izzy, she seems to perk up. She loves babies, and helping me with Izzy makes her feel useful."

"We all need to feel useful." He seemed about to say more, but instead, he swung around and walked out into the main room of the barn.

As she waited for Nana to answer—which could take a while, as the woman had gotten rid of her house phone line but rarely remembered to keep her pre-paid cell phone at her side—she watched Reese walk around to the groups of boys and then over to a simple wooden shelf on a work bench. One of the more solitary boys, Jericho, had drifted over to study it. As Gabby watched, Reese spoke to the boy and gestured. He seemed to be explaining something about the project. Then he used his amputated arm to hold the shelf steady while he sawed with a jigsaw.

His sleeves were rolled up, and his muscles worked beneath his Henley shirt. He was still one of the best-built men she'd ever seen. He hadn't gone soft at all.

He got the shelf most of the way sawed through, and then the saw slipped, making the cut go uneven. He tensed, then straightened and went about trying to trim the excess wood off.

Even making a simple shelf was hard for him—Reese, who'd been known for his superior, elaborate woodworking. Her heart broke a little.

As she spoke to Nana, who couldn't conceal her worsening cough, and as she made a doctor's appointment for her, she thought about what she'd seen, what she'd said.

It hadn't gone as badly as it might have, and that was because Reese had been gentleman enough not to ask her who Izzy's father was. She had to hope that would continue.

For the rest of the morning, as she listened to the students' half-baked plans and discoveries, she realized anew just what she'd taken on in agreeing to this job and in proposing the Christmas show. It was almost inconceivable that the kids could all work together to pull it off.

Almost as inconceivable as her and Reese working together without old animosities getting in the way.

By the end of the day, Reese felt as tired as he had after a hard training exercise in the military.

The boys were working on their final chores, walking the dogs and getting them fresh water and food. Gabby had gone to make a quick check on her grandmother, who wasn't feeling well, but promised to come back to help with cleanup and planning for tomorrow.

Reese supervised the boys while, internally, he yelled at himself.

He'd acted like a sulky kid, like the very boys he was trying to help. He'd shown enough attitude that it was visible to Gabby.

Come to find out, she hadn't cheated on him after all. Or so she said.

Mostly, he believed her. She'd always been an honest person, and she'd looked straight into his eyes as she told him Izzy had been conceived after she'd gone to college.

She hadn't cheated; she'd broken a promise to wait, but that wasn't as awful of an offense. Lots of people found they couldn't handle a long-distance relationship.

Gabby had seemed like the type to keep her promises, but it had turned out differently. He'd left town on June 30, and Brock had posted a picture of him and Gabby together two days later. She hadn't been the person he'd thought she was.

He hadn't brought that up, because he hadn't trusted himself to handle a discussion about it. He knew his limits.

"Hey, Mr. Reese!" Two of the younger boys came running up to him, dogs leaping at their sides. "We thought of an idea!"

He had to smile at their enthusiasm. "Yeah? What is it?"

"What if we had the baby Jesus come into the stable in a spaceship?"

"Yeah, and Mary and Joseph could be dressed up like Transformers!"

Reese tried to keep the dismay he felt inside from showing on his face. It was the best idea he'd heard from the boys all day, and it was awful. Why had they ever pinned their funding to a Christmas show?

"Hmm," he said. "I'm going to have to think about that one."

"He's thinking about it!" they yelled as they took off for the milling crowd of boys and dogs.

Reese sighed, then stood and walked closer to the boys. "Okay, everyone," he called, "let's all work together to get these pups back to their kennels. It's almost time to pack up and go home."

As the boys worked to get the dogs settled for the evening, the door opened. Gabby was back, and… He swallowed. She was carrying her child in a carrier on her chest, the baby facing out. She shut the door behind her and then leaned closer to the baby, murmuring as she loosened her little coat and hat.

Memories he'd long shoved aside rushed back into his mind. He and Gabby had talked about kids, how they both wanted them, how they wanted to raise them better than they'd been raised themselves. They hadn't exactly discussed getting married and raising kids together—they'd both known they were too young for a plan like that—but it had been in the back of his mind, and he'd thought it was in hers, too.

Instead, she'd gone on to become a mother without him. As it turned out, she hadn't been too young at all.

Telling himself to man up wouldn't work. He strode over to her. "Everything's done," he said without looking closely at the baby. "You didn't need to come back."

"Are you upset because I brought her?" Her question was quiet but somehow forceful.

He opened his mouth to deny it, then closed it again and looked off to the side. "I'm working on it, okay? Just…give me a little time."

"Reese."

"Yeah?" He looked back at her.

Her eyes were wide and clear, studying him. "Time as in, until tomorrow? Or time as in, I should forget about working here anymore?"

He *didn't* want her working here, not really, but he didn't want her to leave, either. "I'll be fine tomorrow," he heard himself promise. "I need you if we're going to pull together a show. Be thinking of ideas how to make it work, because unless you love the idea of Jesus arriving by spaceship, we have a ways to go."

"Jesus arriving by…" She giggled, her face breaking into a smile that dazzled him. Maybe even more than when he was a high school kid. "Will do," she said with a comical little salute. Then she kissed the top of the baby's head—devastating Reese all over again—turned and walked out of the barn.

An hour later, Reese was hauling supplies from his truck to the barn when Corbin Beck drove up and parked beside Reese's truck. Reese and the animal science professor had become friends through working together on some repairs at the church. Now Corbin was doing a research study on some of the dogs at Rescue Haven.

"Need a hand?" Corbin asked. "Or… Oh, man, I'm sorry. Wrong thing to say."

Puzzled, Reese looked up, saw that his friend's face had gone red and realized the problem. He smacked Corbin's arm with his prosthesis, lightly. "Don't worry about it. People say that kind of thing all the time. I say it myself."

"I wasn't thinking." Corbin shook his head. "Typical for me. Social skills of a gnat."

"No sweat. I knew what you meant." Reese couldn't get offended about all the references to hands in common conversation, or he'd be mad all the time. "And yes, I could use a hand with moving this stuff."

"Sure thing."

Corbin took the other end of a case of dog food and they hauled it, then another, into the storage area of the barn, chatting mildly about the low temperatures expected for tomorrow and how to manage the dogs in the weather.

"Our boys will be here, cold or not, for the most part," Reese said. "Their parents don't get off work for cold, so they still need places for their kids to go. We'll keep them warm and active here."

"Some of the dogs might benefit from boots to protect their paw pads, and the short-haired guys could use coats. Don't leave them out too long, either."

Reese sighed. "Cabin fever. Just what we need."

"I don't know how you do it," Corbin said. "Kids are a mystery to me."

"I'm no expert. I'm usually winging it to some degree."

It was nearly dark by the time they got everything into the barn and stacked in the supply room. The air was cold enough to bite his face, but Reese felt warm from the exertion. "Thanks," he said. "Couldn't have gotten this done so fast without you."

"No problem," Corbin said as he knelt in front of one of the pens, tablet computer in hand. "Did I hear right that you have a new helper?"

"How'd you hear that?"

"It's a small town." Corbin opened the pen, and Moose, an ancient rottweiler mix, offered a tail wag. "Hey, buddy, how's the leg?"

Reese sat stewing while Corbin examined the dog and typed notes into his computer. Corbin's research had to do with nutritional biology across species, so he was feeding some of the dogs a special food and measuring the effect on the growth of their fatty tumors. "What else did you hear?" Reese asked, noticing the truculence in his voice but unable to govern it.

"Heard she has a baby." Corbin glanced at him and then ducked his head and moved along to the next pen. "Speculation is, it's yours."

"What?" Reese stared at Corbin. "Are you kidding me?"

"Wouldn't kid about something like that."

Reese's mind spun. Since he'd heard Izzy crying at Nana's house, he'd been thinking almost nonstop about the fact that Gabby had a baby, but it had never occurred to him that people might suspect it was his.

"I guess, with her working for you, and with your history together, it was kind of a natural leap." Corbin glanced up from his tablet. "I take it there's no truth to the rumor."

"None." Reese was putting it all together in his own mind. Unless people knew that Izzy had been premature, which wasn't at all obvious when you looked at her, the math would work out for her being conceived while Reese and Gabby were dating.

It was the conclusion he'd jumped to himself.

What other people didn't know was that he and Gabby hadn't been intimate. In this day and age, their abstinence would be unexpected.

Corbin glanced at him again, eyebrows raised.

"We never…" He stopped, then tried again. "We agreed not to…"

"I get it," Corbin said. "I'm impressed. Can't have been easy."

"Izzy was born prematurely," Reese went on, working it out in his own mind as he spoke. "Gabby told me that, and I believe her."

Corbin nodded. He was stroking one of the older, more fearful dogs, Bundi, gently on the chest. "Hey, Bundi, girl," he whispered, using the correct pronunciation, *Boon-dee*.

Corbin was meticulous. And usually right.

"I guess Gabby changed after a couple years of college," Reese said, feeling bleak.

"It can happen." Corbin scratched under the dog's chin, and she rolled onto her back in response. "How do you feel about it?"

"I'm upset. But I know I shouldn't be. Like you said, it happens. Happens to a lot of people."

"You're allowed to be mad," Corbin said with a little smile quirking the corner of his mouth. "We're all

sinners in need of grace. She got together with someone right after you guys separated. You're mad about
it. It's a fallen world and we're fallen people."

It was the most he'd heard quiet Corbin say all at
once, and maybe for that reason, Reese took it seriously.

The man was right. Gabby had made a mistake.
Reese had gotten mad about it. Both of those things
were natural, people being what they were, and that
meant they could get past them.

Important, because they needed to work together
to make sure some troubled boys and high-risk dogs
had a place where they could get the help they needed.

Chapter Five

The next day, a Tuesday, Gabby, the boys and Biff, the giant black dog Jacob was training, climbed out of the van in front of Cleo's Crafts and Café. Reese pulled into a parking space—town was crowded with Christmas shoppers, apparently—while Gabby reminded the boys about good behavior. They'd called ahead to clear the visit with Cleo, but still…ten big teen and preteen boys in a craft shop was a lot.

Jacob started in with the rest, but she tapped his shoulder. "Someone has to stay outside with Biff," she reminded him.

"It says it's dog friendly." He pointed at a sign.

"That's only if your dog is well behaved. Maybe one day, Biff will be able to go in, but not until he's reliable with the basics and doesn't jump on people."

Jacob opened his mouth as if to argue, but Biff chose that moment to lunge at a gray-haired woman and her Chihuahua walking past, the Chihuahua decked out in a pink sweater and cap. Fortunately, between them, Gabby and Jacob were able to restrain Biff, but not before a major barkfest. Biff's deep bass woofs and the Chihuahua's soprano ones drew attention from passersby.

Fortunately, the Chihuahua's owner didn't get upset; she laughed, picked up her yapping dog and patted Biff's head. "Merry Christmas from both of us," she said, waving the Chihuahua's paw at them before turning and walking away.

"Biff is strong," Jacob admitted after the woman and dog had walked on down the street. "I'll stay outside and work on his training. See, I brought treats." He held up a bag.

"You think you can control him?"

"Yeah. He just caught me off guard that time. Right, Biff?" He knelt and put an arm around the big dog.

Biff gave a low woof and licked Jacob's face, and Jacob laughed and rubbed the dog's floppy ears, then kissed his head. It was an unscripted, vulnerable moment in which Gabby saw her brother for the child he still was.

Working with Biff was so good for Jacob. It was bringing out a side of him she hadn't seen before, a side that touched her heart. She couldn't resist bending down to rub Jacob's arm, moving away before he could protest. She didn't want to push it.

As she started into the store, Reese arrived from parking the van and fell into step beside her. "You really care for him, don't you?"

She glanced back at Jacob, who was using a treat to try to guide Biff into a sit as the dog cocked his head, looking puzzled. "Yeah. I'm sorry to say I barely knew him when he was younger. Just no opportunity. Having him here for the holidays is a blessing."

"For both of you."

"And for Nana, too," she said. "Jacob is a good kid. He might act uninterested in stuff, but he spent a couple of hours watching YouTube videos on dog training last night. He wants to do a good job."

Reese's mouth quirked into a smile. "Hope it works. Biff is a tough case."

"I appreciate your giving him a challenge. It's just what he needs."

"Fifteen is a tough age." As they went inside, he gestured at the rest of the boys, clustered at the other side of the shop. "So you think their idea is going to work?"

"You're being generous, calling it an idea. It's pretty rough."

"It's all we've got."

"True." She studied the boys. Hair sticking up or flattened down, all arms and legs and big feet, making too much noise for the small shop. "To be honest, I have no idea. But I think dressing up the dogs as stable animals in the nativity could be cute."

He grimaced. "Dogs in outfits never appealed to me."

"It's not outfits, exactly," she consoled him as they approached the boys. "More…costumes. Like for actors."

"Do you have time to make all those costumes?"

She lifted an eyebrow. "I'm not making them. I'm teaching the boys how to sew, and they're making them."

"In a *week*?" The words seemed to burst out of him.

"Chill, Reese!" She patted his arm. "It won't take that long."

He looked up at the ceiling and blew out a breath,

then looked back at her. "Gabby, I don't know if you realize how serious this is. If Santiago Romano talks the board into pulling our funding, the program will end and these kids won't have anywhere to go." He glanced back toward the street where Jacob was working with Biff. "The dogs, too."

She slightly resented the accusation that she wasn't taking it seriously, but on the other hand, he had a point. She was new, here temporarily, not as invested in the program as he was. She'd come up with the idea of the Christmas pageant and blurted it out without really thinking it through. "I'm sorry, Reese," she said, touching the fabric of his shirt sleeve to keep his attention, feeling the hard prosthesis beneath her fingers. "I won't take it lightly. The costumes will get made, and I'll do my very best to make the program a success."

He'd stopped still when she'd touched him, and now he glanced down at where her hand still rested on his prosthetic arm. They were blocked off from the boys by a Christmas tree decorated with colorful ceramic ornaments. The smell of evergreen pine blended with a ginger and cinnamon fragrance from the café side. The boys were talking quietly and laughing, and in the background, quiet Christmas music played.

She made the mistake of looking into Reese's eyes, and then she couldn't look away.

He was watching her with eyes narrowed, his expression speculative. It was the Reese she'd known and loved in high school, and yet it wasn't. These eyes had seen war and pain and loss. They had a depth of understanding that hadn't been there before.

She sucked in a breath, her palms suddenly moist, her heart dancing along at a faster-than-normal clip.

If they were alone, she'd have been sorely tempted to reach up and pull him closer for a kiss.

Did he still feel the chemistry between them?

Suddenly, from the other side of the Christmas display where the boys were gathered, a loud, discordant rap song blared out, its beat throbbing, questionable lyrics penetrating the peace of the little shop.

"Whoa!" Gabby looked away from Reese and saw an older gentleman among the woodworking supplies, frowning and touching his hearing aid.

"Let's put a stop to that right now," Reese said.

They both rushed over to the boys, but it was Reese's stern voice that got their attention. "Turn that off. Now."

"Aw, it's a great song." Wolf, the biggest of the boys, put a pleading tone into his voice, but after another look at Reese's expression, he turned off the music.

"We're in a public place with its own music," Gabby scolded. "You can't be playing yours."

"We're just trying to find the background music of a couple of songs we might use," David said. He was the one who'd been fighting with Wolf on the day she'd interviewed, and she was glad to see they were getting along, for now at least.

"We're making up our own words and putting it to music, a song that we already know," another boy, Connor from the train station, chimed in.

"Kinda like karaoke, only more creative," David added.

"Is that even legal?" Reese asked, frowning. "We don't want to use an artist's music without paying for it."

"We'll research it," Gabby said. "I'm pretty sure

there are websites where you can download music for free or cheap."

She looked at Reese, who stood, hands on hips, looking too large for the cute little shop. He also seemed more cautious, more guarded, more of a worrier than the free-spirited boy she'd known in high school and during the carefree years afterwards.

It wasn't her place to judge him, though. He had all kinds of reasons for his attitude to have darkened.

Meanwhile, it looked like she needed to take charge. "I need two or three of you to come look at fabric," she said briskly, "and I'll show you how to measure it and make sure you have the right amount. The rest of you..." She looked at Reese. "The rest of you can order hot chocolate and Christmas cookies for all of us over in the café. Find a couple of big tables and start writing down your ideas for the show. If that song you were playing is part of it, explain your vision to Reese. *Without* playing it again in here."

As she started to walk away, she felt Reese's touch on her shoulder and paused, looking back.

"Thanks," he said, "and I'm sorry to be a grouch. I'll work on my attitude."

His smile was so dazzling, she was rendered speechless. She opened and closed her mouth, couldn't find words, then turned around and followed the boys to the bolts of fabric.

Working with Reese meant they saw each other at their best and their worst, and that they were forced to communicate.

And her own fluttery feelings for him might make their togetherness more complicated than she'd ever expected.

* * *

Half an hour later, Reese stirred the last of his hot chocolate with a peppermint stick and watched Gabby give feedback to the boys on the lyrics they were working on. She was good with them, gently steering them away from words and phrases that might offend, praising the few promising portions. She laughed at their jokes, a husky sound that danced along his nerve endings, and when she looked over at him and smiled, her whole face lit up.

He didn't feel very optimistic, still, about the production, but at least he felt like there would be *some* kind of show. And working with Gabby on it was… interesting.

Just as she got the boys started on some revisions, her phone buzzed. She looked at the text with concern, then smiled.

"Good news?" he asked her.

She nodded. "Nana's doctor is actually an old acquaintance of mine. Remember Sheniqua Rhoades?"

He got an image of a smiling older girl in long, beaded braids. "Sort of."

"It was that program where college girls helped out at the middle school. She was my mentor. Anyway, she says Nana's going to be fine." She glanced at the message again. "As long as she can rest and not get stressed."

"Rest and not get stressed? Taking care of…" He bit off the rest of his sentence, not wanting to make her feel bad.

She read his mind. Just like she always had. "I know," she said. "How can she relax while taking care of Izzy? But I truly think she enjoys it, and she knows she can always call me to take her if it gets to be too much." She looked up at him from underneath her bangs. "That's okay with you, right? If I bring her over to work every now and then? Or not?"

"It's fine," he said firmly. He'd done a lot of thinking and praying after talking with Corbin last night. He'd realized he had some growing to do, and maybe the way that was going to happen was through Gabby and her daughter.

Nobody was perfect. Which meant he didn't have to be, either.

Their eyes met and held, and then she looked away, staring out the window. Then her brow wrinkled. "Who's that girl Jacob's talking to? She looks familiar."

Reese followed her line of sight. "That's trouble," he said, standing. "She's my cousin."

"That's Paige? Brock's baby sister?"

Reese nodded. "Yep."

Some of the kids around them picked up on their conversation and focus. "That must be Jacob's friend he was talking about," David said.

"He's gonna ask her to be the Virgin Mary," Connor said. "Because none of us wanted to play a girl."

"She's hot." A grin spread across Wolf's face.

"Hey, now," Reese said. "That's my cousin, and you're only allowed to admire her mind. She's very smart."

A smile quirked up the corners of Gabby's mouth, but it quickly turned to a frown. "Oh, no. Is that your aunt and uncle?"

Reese turned and then stood. "I'll deal with them, but you might want to come help with Jacob."

"I will." She looked severely at the boys. "Wolf,

you're in charge of keeping everyone neat and quiet while we talk to the Markowskis. I want to see those lyrics revised and sketches of the costumes when we come back, so get busy, all of you."

Reese was glad she'd thought of giving the boys a task, but even more, he was determined to get to Jacob and Paige before his aunt and uncle started trouble.

But he was too late. Just as he stepped outside, Biff lifted a muddy paw in the direction of his aunt, getting mud on her cream-colored coat.

"Eek!" she screeched. "Get that beast away from me."

Jacob knelt, rubbing Biff's ears. "You gave paw, boy! Good job!"

"It most certainly was *not* a good job," his aunt sputtered.

"Oh, Mom," Paige said. "He didn't hurt you, and anyway, wearing a light-colored coat in all this slush is ridiculous."

"It is, dear," Reese's uncle said. "But," he added, glaring at Paige, "we've discussed this before. You're not to have any contact with that boy." He nodded dismissively toward Jacob.

Gabby took a step forward and put an arm around Jacob's shoulders. He didn't shrug away, which spoke volumes about how upset he was.

Reese had been in Jacob's shoes, the bad kid nobody wanted around, and he felt for the boy. He just wasn't sure whether it was worth it to try to fix a relationship that was never going to work out. Probably best to just keep Jacob away from his aunt and uncle, who weren't going to change.

"Da-ad," Paige whined, "you made me block him on social, but you didn't say I couldn't even talk to him."

"I'm saying it now. There's nothing you two need to talk about."

"Yes, there is! They want me to be the Virgin Mary in their Christmas pageant." Paige grabbed her father's hand. "Can I, Daddy, please?"

"I don't think it's a good..." He sputtered to a stop and looked at his wife. "Mother? What do you think?"

"I think someone should help me clean off this coat," she said. She was rubbing at the muddy paw print with a tissue. It looked like she was making it worse.

Nowhere in the whole conversation had either of them acknowledged Reese, but he still felt obliged to intervene. "Listen, everyone. This doesn't have to be decided now, here, in the cold." He turned to Jacob. "If Paige can't do it, there are several other girls from the church who could."

"Mom! I want to do it. I'd be the only girl."

Reese looked over at Gabby, who gave him a minuscule shrug. Jacob was kneeling beside Biff, restraining him from jumping...and also getting some comfort from the big dog's slobbery, unconditional love, Reese was guessing.

"Reese," Gabby said, "if you could hold Biff, I'd like for Jacob to go inside with me. I need to take a look at what the other boys are working on, and Jacob needs to get up to speed with them, as well."

And we both need to get away from your toxic aunt and uncle. He could read that unspoken message.

"Good idea," he said, and took the leash from Jacob. Once the two of them were inside, any hint of civility disappeared from Paige's voice. "You embarrassed me so much!" She glared at her parents. "How could you be so rude to him?"

"That boy is trouble," Reese's uncle said.

"He's doing his best." Reese was reaching for patience. "I'm going to leave the three of you to discuss whether Paige can participate. If she can't, I understand, but if you could let us know ASAP, we'd appreciate it."

Uncle Clive's eyes narrowed. "Just what's the connection between you and that woman?" He gestured in Gabby's direction.

Reese lifted an eyebrow. "She's my employee."

"And that's all?"

"That's all." Reese was only now realizing he wished it could be more.

"Let us talk about it," Aunt Catherine suggested unexpectedly. She pulled her husband's sleeve, practically dragging him off to the side of the store building.

Then commenced a vehement discussion out of their hearing. Paige and Reese watched for a minute.

"How's school?" he asked, trying for normal conversation.

"We're on break." She frowned toward her parents. "I just don't get why they're so against Jacob. When I started hanging out with him last summer, they acted like he was a criminal. But as far as I know, he hasn't ever gotten into any real trouble."

"Just not their kind of people, I guess."

"Like you were?" Paige looked at him shrewdly.

"Touché." He looked through the window and was relieved to see that Gabby and the boys were smiling and talking. Nobody seemed upset; nobody seemed to be getting out of hand.

"We've made a decision," Uncle Clive said as he and Aunt Catherine came back toward them.

"I can't wait," Paige muttered.

"She may do the show," Aunt Catherine said, grandly, as if bestowing an enormous favor, "but Clive or I will be at every rehearsal."

Reese nearly groaned aloud. It was challenging enough to keep the boys on track and to prioritize which of their poor manners or bad language to correct. With his aunt and uncle there, they'd all be under pressure to be perfect.

Not only that, but Gabby would be under constant scrutiny, and Aunt Catherine in particular would be looking for opportunities to criticize her. Reese already felt defensive on her behalf.

The remaining rehearsals were going to be doubly stressful, and none of them needed that.

Chapter Six

Two days later—two days closer to showtime—Gabby heard a car pull up outside the barn. She checked the time on her phone and groaned inside. They weren't close to ready for the Markowskis to arrive.

The barn was strewn with coats and boots and dog toys. The boys were arguing over control of the laptop computer they were composing their songs on. And the sound of car doors slamming got all the dogs barking.

She glanced over at Reese, and as was happening more and more often these days, they communicated without words. Troubleshooting time.

Reese walked toward her, shoulders squared, decisive, a leader. "You hold them off for a few minutes. I want to talk to the boys, man-to-man."

Normally, she would have objected to the sexism of that, but she was willing to try anything.

She walked out the barn door and there were Paige and Mrs. Markowski, arguing in front of the family Mercedes. The expensive cut of Mrs. Markowski's coat, her perfect hair, her designer boots made Gabby conscious of her own shabby jeans and college hoodie.

Paige wore workout clothes from a brand Gabby had heard of but never even aspired to purchase. The teenager's socks probably cost more than Gabby's entire outfit.

She could hear the boys joking and laughing behind her, the sound of Jacob's voice ringing out with the rest. She glanced back and saw her brother smiling, having fun.

That was what was important. Not designer clothes, but a boy finding a place to fit in.

Mrs. Markowski turned and saw her. "We have an hour before Paige's track practice," Mrs. Markowski said without bothering to greet Gabby.

So she wasn't even going to pretend to be friendly. "Well…we'll see what we can get done in that amount of time." Gabby turned and beckoned both of them toward the barn.

"One minute." Mrs. Markowski touched Gabby's arm. "Go on ahead, Paige. I need to talk with Gabby for a few minutes."

Paige shrugged and walked on in, and Gabby turned back toward the older woman. "If you're concerned about Paige being here with the boys, I can assure you that everyone is well supervised. Reese makes sure of that."

"It's not that. I'm actually concerned about *you.*" Mrs. Markowski gave her a tight smile.

Really? Somehow, I don't think so. Gabby stuck her hands into her back pockets and waited.

"I heard a rumor that Reese's old assistant might not come back."

"Really?" Gabby's heart gave a jump, a happy one.

She was liking the work here already, and if there was a chance she could stay on…

"I'm just going to come out and say it. You're not thinking of staying in Bethlehem Springs, are you?"

Now I am. Gabby cocked her head to one side. "Why do you ask?"

Mrs. Markowski's lips pressed together. "It's the gossip, dear. It's terrible. After living in a bigger city, you may have forgotten just how conservative Bethlehem Springs can be."

Understanding was starting to dawn on Gabby, but she needed to know for sure. "Gossip about what?" Was there some way Mrs. Markowski had learned the truth about what had happened the evening her son had been killed?

"About your baby, dear."

Heat climbed Gabby's face and shame knotted her stomach, even though she knew, in her head, that she hadn't done anything wrong. Unless being naive and trusting was a crime.

But how strange was it to be talking to Reese's aunt—Brock's mother, which made her Izzy's grandmother—about her and her baby being an embarrassment to the town?

Her heart pounded as she stared at the woman's hard, cold eyes, an exact match to her son's. Her breathing quickened.

She was about to lose it. Instinctively, she touched the cross necklace she always wore.

God is in control, so you don't have to be.

It was a truth she'd leaned on when her life had gone in a direction she'd never expected. She knew with bone-deep certainty that He could bestow good even after the darkest events. Izzy was living proof of that.

She drew in a breath and let it out slowly. "Thanks for your input," she said, lifting her chin. She wasn't going to get into an argument with the woman, but she also wasn't going to kiss up to her. Who approached a single mom and told her there was gossip about her baby and she should leave town, especially in this day and age? She squared her shoulders and kept breathing deeply as she led the way into the barn.

She refused to worry about what Mrs. Markowski had said, but the woman's question had made her think about something she'd pushed aside until now: Would she stay on after Christmas?

Gossip or not—and she had to suspect some of that was just among Mrs. Markowski's snobbish group of friends, whose opinions didn't really affect Gabby— she found herself liking the idea of staying here. The town really was livable, a nice place for Izzy to grow up. Nana needed Gabby, and that need wouldn't decrease in years to come. And truthfully, Gabby needed Nana, as well. For her wisdom, for her skill with Izzy, for her love. She hadn't realized how lonely she'd felt with no family around until she'd gotten a taste of belonging somewhere again.

Even Jacob was starting to feel like a real brother to her. And if she could keep this job…what could be more perfect? She liked working with the boys. She was nearby if Nana needed her, and she could let Izzy stay with family rather than strangers.

It was all riding on whether they could make the show a success. Which meant not alienating the Markowskis, who were perfectly capable of spreading negative gossip around town and to Mr. Romano, who, according to Nana, traveled in the same wealthy circles they did.

Reese had the kids sitting working together around the table. The boys were being remarkably quiet and respectful, greeting Mrs. Markowski politely and then returning to the papers and computers they were working on.

What had Reese said to them to evoke this kind of great behavior? Regardless of that, and regardless of Mrs. Markowski's rudeness, she needed to swallow her emotions. The past was past, and she had to make this situation work day by day, with God's help.

"Dude," Wolf said, looking at Jacob. "We should get started."

"Right." Jacob cleared his throat and spoke up firmly. "Everyone has their parts. Let's run through it."

Pride pushed past Gabby's worried thoughts. Jacob was assuming a leadership role, which was terrific for him in all kinds of ways.

They all gathered at one end of the barn, clutching papers, jostling each other, giggling nervously.

"What about the animals?" one of the younger boys yelled. "Don't they have to practice, too?"

"Let's get the people parts going well first," Reese suggested, the hint of a smile on his face.

"And…music!" Jacob pointed at another of the younger boys, who fiddled with a phone and computer. Suddenly, booming music with a heavy bass beat filled the barn. Several dogs started barking, and all three adults clapped their hands to their ears. "Turn it down!" Reese ordered, and after a minute, the boy did as he'd asked.

"Okay, now I'll point to you when it's time to come in," Jacob said.

They proceeded to go through a very rough and very colorful version of the nativity story, all done more or less to the tune of three different rap songs that had been popular last year. It was so ragged that Gabby couldn't imagine how it would get to a point where they could do the performance in front of the congregation. Reese's aunt was shaking her head, her mouth twisting to one side.

Paige looked around at the boys and put her hands on her hips. "For one thing, everyone has to learn their parts. You all need to get ahold of the music and practice when you come in, before tomorrow's rehearsal. Tyler," she said, pointing to the boy who'd done the music, "could you list everyone in order?"

"We could just print out the whole thing, and then everyone could highlight their own lines," Jacob suggested.

"Good idea. The other thing is, we should include some regular Christmas carols mixed in with the rap. Like, a different one after each song."

Wolf frowned. "That'll make it boring."

"Maybe to you," Paige said, "but the people in the audience are old. They'll like it."

Gabby looked over at Reese, who was barely suppressing a smile. "Who are they calling old?" she asked in a whisper.

"To a bunch of teenagers, we *are* old," he said ruefully. "And I'd like Christmas carols a million times better than the songs they're using."

"People like to participate, to be involved," Paige lectured on. "And besides, the show is going to be too short otherwise."

"Good point," Jacob said. He was staring at Paige with an awestruck smile, the picture of puppy love.

"Let's go through it once more," she said, and then looked at Jacob. "Is that okay?"

He grinned, nodded and then pointed at the music boy. "From the top."

This time was marginally better. The boys seemed to be taking it more seriously because Paige was.

"Now, you guys work in some Christmas carols. Nothing weird, just the regular ones like 'Hark the Herald Angels Sing,' got it?"

"Got it," they chorused.

"All right. I have to go to track practice, but I'll be back tomorrow at the same time to go through it all again." With a wave, she waltzed out of the barn.

Mrs. Markowski stood, too, and Reese and Gabby walked her out. "Your daughter is a good leader," Gabby said.

Reese laughed. "She comes by it naturally, right, Aunt Catherine?"

But Mrs. Markowski didn't smile. "I don't seem to have been successful letting Gabby know about the gossip in town," she said, "so I'll tell you, Reese. Everyone's talking about that baby of hers. And this can't help your reputation—most people are saying it's yours."

His aunt's words weren't a shock to Reese—he'd heard the same from Corbin—but they still hit him hard, and he instantly looked at Gabby. Her hand was over her mouth, unshed tears in her eyes. She was staring at his aunt's retreating back, for she'd thrown that little volley and left the battleground.

His body tensed, his muscles quivering, fists

clenching. No one should be gossiping about Gabby, but even if gossip was inevitable, there was no need for his aunt to upset her with it.

He started after his aunt. "That was inappropriate," he called after her. "I don't need to hear gossip and neither does—"

"Reese." Gabby's hand was on his arm, clutching his sleeve. "Let them go. Paige and the boys don't need to hear all of this."

"But she has no right—" He broke off and turned back to her. "You have a point. This isn't the time or place to talk with her about it."

"She's not going to change." Gabby sighed. "And what she's saying, I'm sure she didn't make it up. I'm so sorry your name is getting mixed up in the gossip about me."

The Mercedes roared off, spinning gravel. His aunt was at the wheel, a mean little smile on her face.

"I apologize for my family," he said. "What did she say to you before?"

"That I should leave town to keep gossip from building." She frowned. "Maybe I ought to."

The thought of Gabby leaving hit him harder than it should have, but there wasn't time to process it. A couple of cars pulled up, Wolf's dad picking up Wolf and another boy, then David's mom. The other parents would be here for pickup soon, so Reese and Gabby walked inside to help the rest of the boys gather their things and clean up.

Gabby looked at the clock and bit her lip.

"Do you need to head out?" he asked, concerned for her. "I can take it from here. I'm sure Nana would welcome a break."

"I'm sure she would," Gabby said, "but I have to

grocery shop. There's nothing, and I mean nothing, for dinner." She laughed a little. "To tell you the truth, I'm not used to cooking for a family. I have no idea what I'm going to make."

That was when he realized what an adjustment she was facing. New job, new living situation that involved some caregiving for Nana, and the sudden addition of Jacob to the mix.

She never complained, but looking at her eyes, he read the tiredness there. "Tell you what," he said, inspired, "let me do the grocery shopping. Nana had been giving me a list for a few weeks, while she was sick, but she stopped when you arrived. I'll shop if you'll stay with the rest of the boys until their rides arrive. Then you can go home with Jacob and chill a little. I'll come over with the groceries and cook dinner for you guys."

"But why would you—"

"I want to help," he said. "And we should talk about what to do about Aunt Catherine, but talking will go down easier once we've had some food. I assume everyone goes to bed early, so maybe we can have some privacy."

She bit her lip and looked up at him, her cheeks going pink.

He realized how his remark had sounded. "I didn't mean that kind of privacy—I meant, to talk."

"Of course," she said, still blushing, looking away. "If you're sure, that would be a big help."

Two hours later, they were all sitting around Nana's table: Reese, Gabby, Nana, Jacob and baby Izzy, who was in a high chair at the corner of the table between Jacob and Gabby.

"This looks great!" Jacob stuffed a big bite of pasta into his mouth.

"Jacob!" Both Nana and Gabby scolded at the same time. "Prayers first."

"And because you're so eager, you can say it," Nana added with a wink to Reese.

They all bowed their heads and took each other's hands. Nana's, on his left, was thin, bones covered by papery skin.

Gabby was on his right, and he was wearing the prosthetic he favored when he needed to get things done, the pincerlike claw. It was functional, but not exactly pleasing to the eye. He looked over at her doubtfully.

She was waiting, one eyebrow lifted. "I'd like to hold your hand," she said simply.

He held out his prosthetic, and she took it and bowed her head.

"Thank You, Lord, for these Thy gifts which we are about to receive in Jesus's name, amen," Jacob said in a rush.

"Amen." He heard a suppressed laugh in Gabby's voice and she glanced over at him with merriment in her eyes. As she shifted in her chair, the side of her leg brushed against his.

He felt the physical contact like a jolt of electricity coursing through his body.

"Now we can eat," Nana said, "and this pasta smells terrific. I like a man who can cook."

"So do I," Gabby said so softly that he couldn't be sure she'd really said it.

This spontaneously offered dinner, however non-romantically he'd meant it, might have been a terrible mistake. He didn't want to be having the feelings he was having. Shouldn't, because Gabby had dumped him once before. He couldn't open himself up to it happening again. Couldn't trust that the small, unconsciously flirtatious things she did meant anything.

They all dug in. Pickles jumped up onto the table, and when Gabby put him firmly back down, he hissed at her, cementing his sour reputation.

Biff ambled over and put a giant paw on the cat. Not hurting him, just holding him to the floor.

"He wants Mr. Pickles to apologize!" Jacob said as the cat meowed indignantly.

"It's okay, Biff, thank you," Gabby said, patting the dog and laughing, and Biff let the cat up and sat beside Gabby, panting up at her.

It was an attitude Reese could totally understand. Gabby was flushed, smiling, having fun, and she was enormously appealing.

"This happens every night," Nana explained. "It's a turf war between Biff and Mr. Pickles."

As if to illustrate her point, Biff sniffed at Mr. Pickles, and the cat batted his nose. Biff reared back and sat down, and the cat walked off at a deliberate pace, tail twitching.

Biff had come home from the barn to sleep. Apparently, they'd been bringing him home every night "to socialize him," but it was looking like the big, out-of-control dog was becoming a part of their family.

"So, Jacob," Reese said, trying to distract himself from the sight, sound and overall very appealing presence of Gabby, "what did you think about Paige's contribution to the project?"

"She's awesome." Jacob said it through a mouthful and continued eating.

"She *was* pretty awesome." Gabby explained the rehearsal to Nana.

Nana laughed, obviously enjoying the description. "Any event like that is better if a woman's involved in the planning."

"Hey," Reese protested, "are you saying men can't organize a show? Men can do anything! Just look at this meal." He was joking around. "Stand up for me here, Jacob. Mr. Pickles."

The cat, seeming to recognize his name, gave a loud, annoyed meow, making them all laugh.

Jacob nodded. "The guys can figure it out eventually, but Paige can do it faster. She had good ideas." He looked slyly at Gabby. "See, I'm focusing on her brain and not her looks."

Gabby fist-bumped him. "Good, good. You're improving."

Izzy had been watching them all with round eyes, very much like Gabby's. "Guh, guh," she said, banging her cup on her high chair tray for emphasis.

"New word! She said *good*!" Gabby sounded joyful.

"Want me to write it down?" Jacob offered. Without waiting for an answer, he swiped a napkin across his mouth and went to the chalkboard on one side of the kitchen. Reese saw now that there was a list of words there.

"Good, good," Gabby cooed. "Such a good baby. So smart!" She dropped a kiss on Izzy's forehead.

Reese's heart twisted.

She loved her baby, that much was clear. And she was trying her best to manage as a single mom, which couldn't be easy. Gabby's family had never had much money, and looking around the shabby kitchen, he knew nothing had changed on the financial side.

His aunt's voice echoed in his mind. *"People think she's yours."*

Did people really think that? Should he and Gabby try to disabuse folks of the notion?

Who *was* Izzy's father?

After a few more minutes around the table, with Jacob telling ridiculous stories about the boys and dogs, Nana adjourned to her room and Jacob to his to play video games. Gabby excused herself to put Izzy to bed.

Reese started carrying dishes to the kitchen, humming a little, stepping carefully over Pickles, who'd chosen this moment to weave in and out between Reese's feet, purring and rubbing for attention.

"Now you get friendly," he said to the cat. He filled the sink with soapy water and started scraping and rinsing plates before plunging them in.

Pickles meowed up at him.

"What's wrong, buddy? Is it dinnertime?" He spotted a pouch of cat treats on the counter and knelt to hand a couple to the cat.

Pickles gobbled them down while Reese petted him and then meowed again.

"Not so sour now, are ya?" He dropped more treats onto the floor.

"Talking to the cat?" Gabby asked from the doorway, sounding amused.

"Maybe." He looked up at her and sucked in his breath. She looked so happy and relaxed in her sweater and jeans, hair loose around her shoulders, more like a high school kid than a mother and caregiver.

Their eyes met and held for a moment, and then

she looked away, her cheeks heating. "You don't have to do the dishes," she said, walking over to the sink. "You cooked. I'll clean up."

"I made a mess. Wasn't thinking about how Nana doesn't have a dishwasher." He nodded toward the dish towel. "I'm running out of space in the dish rack. You can dry dishes and put them away."

"If you're sure. You must be tired, though."

He shook his head. "Not really. Besides, we should talk."

"Yeah." She dried plates and stacked them in the cupboard. "I'm sorry people are gossiping, Reese. You don't deserve to be included in that."

"Neither do you," he said. "Nobody deserves to be the target of petty gossip."

"Thanks," she said, "but at least I'm the actual parent of the kid in question." Her cheeks went even pinker. "You're not involved at all, and there's no reason for our names to be linked together."

"I'm not even sure there is gossip," Reese said. "Or at least, I'm not sure that it's widespread. This isn't really a gossipy town."

"Most of the time, no. But I have a bit of a reputation already."

"Because of how you were as kid and teen?" She'd been a little wild, no doubt. She'd dressed differently from the other kids, which was economic, but she'd made it seem like a choice.

"Yeah, that. And…yeah. That."

She'd been going to say something else, and he wanted to know what it was, but he didn't want to pry. He took another angle. "I hope it's not going to push you into leaving town."

She glanced toward the back of the house, where quiet noise came from Nana's television and Jacob's video game. "I didn't intend to stay past Christmas," she said. "But now that I'm here, I see how Nana needs me."

"Jacob seems at home, too," he said.

"I know, and he loves Izzy. He's so excited to be Uncle Jacob."

"It's good for him."

"I'd like to stay and figure out a way to keep him here," she said. "But I don't know. Your aunt made it sound really bad, like I shouldn't stay."

"Did you ever let someone like that govern your life before?"

"Once." Her face darkened and her eyes went far away.

He wondered what was going through her mind. "Want to talk about it?"

She shook her head rapidly and dried her hands on the dish towel.

Now he was *really* curious. Did she mean the father of her baby?

He had to think the guy had taken advantage of her. And what kind of jerk wouldn't be involved in his baby's life, no matter what had happened between him and the mother? What kind of jerk would he have to be to have Gabby bar him from Izzy's life? He was pretty sure she wouldn't do that capriciously.

She brushed her hands together and looked around, avoiding his eyes. "We just have to do a little wiping up. And figure out what to do about all this gossip."

He grabbed a cloth and started wiping down counters. "I don't think there's anything we can do. We're working together, and that could contribute."

"You're not thinking of letting me go?"

"No." He stopped his cleaning and turned to face her. "Because I don't let my aunt dictate my life, either. Gabby, you're doing a great job and I'd actually like to keep you on full-time after Christmas if the money comes through." Then he could have kicked himself. He hadn't thought about the offer; it had come up spontaneously.

She tilted her head to one side and looked up at him, studying him. "Why are you offering me that? Because you feel sorry for me?"

"Because I need you and we work well together." And he felt like they were having a double conversation here. He was talking about the Rescue Haven program, yes, but there was a personal thread, too.

She bit her lip. "I've been thinking how good the job is for my whole…situation. If you're serious about extending it after Christmas, I'd definitely be interested."

He wanted to probe into what she'd said. Did her interest have something to do with him, personally, or was it only the convenience of the job?

But he wouldn't push. She'd rejected him once before, and he'd been a whole man then. Now he was disabled. He didn't know how a woman would react to a romantic overture from a man with a hook instead of a hand. He knew he was no less a man, and he wasn't ashamed of how he looked, but you couldn't deny that physical stuff was important in romantic relationships. If his body repulsed her, then no amount of thinking or wishing or talking was going to make things work.

She wiped a counter that he'd already wiped clean. "Thanks for fixing dinner for us tonight," she said, not looking at him. "It meant a lot to Nana and Jacob.

To all of us, but especially me. It was fun to have the help."

"Anytime," he said lightly. And, precisely because he didn't want to leave, he dried off and went to the coatrack. "I should get on home, leave you to relax in peace."

"Sure. I understand." The words sounded a little bit plaintive, and for the first time, he realized that she might be lonely in the evenings. A baby, a teenage boy and an older woman, no matter how beloved, weren't much company after seven or eight o'clock.

He reached out a hand, meaning to shake hers, but she grasped his and held it. Looked into his eyes. "Reese, I'm sorry about what happened before."

He narrowed his eyes and frowned at her. "You mean…after I went into the service?"

She nodded and swallowed hard. "Something happened, and I couldn't… I couldn't keep the promise I made."

That something being another guy, Izzy's father. He drew in a breath. Was he going to hold on to his grudge, or his hurt feelings, about what had happened?

Looking into her eyes, he breathed out the last of his anger. Like Corbin had said, everyone was a sinner. "It's understood."

"Thank you," she said simply. She held his gaze for another moment and then looked down and away.

She was still holding on to his hand, and slowly, he twisted and opened his hand until their palms were flat together. Pressed between them as close as he'd like to be pressed to Gabby.

The only light in the room came from the kitchen and the dying fire. Outside the windows, snow had started to fall, blanketing the little house in solitude.

This night with her family had been one of the best he'd had in a long time. Made him realize how much he missed having a family. Even made him think of the long-ago days when his parents were alive. Memories of his childhood were a little dim, but he knew his parents had agreed to endless board games and jigsaw puzzles, sometimes with just Reese and sometimes with friends he'd invited over. His mom, especially, had known what it was like to be an only child, because she'd been one, too. She'd insisted that they make a special effort to give him the attention and companionship he'd missed by not having siblings.

That had all changed on the fateful day of their accident. They'd been a close family and then, boom, it was gone. Reeling and stunned, he'd been sent to live with his aunt and uncle and Brock, whom he'd barely known apart from a few awkward holiday gatherings.

Uncle Clive and Aunt Catherine and Brock hadn't spent their evenings playing board games. They'd all watched TV in separate rooms or gone out to be with separate friends. Even once Paige had arrived, the new baby hadn't brought them all together. Brock had resented the intrusion and Uncle Clive had gotten busier at work. Aunt Catherine tried, but he'd seen her cringe away from the noise and mess of a baby.

As for Reese, he'd tried to lay low and hang on, distracting himself from his losses with sports. He'd tried to play with Paige some—as she grew, she was the warmest member of the family by far—but he wished he'd done more.

He'd known, even then, that he couldn't fix a family that dysfunctional.

It had been so long since he'd been part of a real,

good family that he'd forgotten he wanted it. Tonight, he'd regained that desire.

Gabby's hand against his felt small and delicate, but he knew better. He slipped his own hand to the side and captured hers, tracing his thumb along the calluses.

He heard her breath hitch and looked quickly at her face.

Her eyes were wide, her lips parted and moist.

Without looking away, acting on impulse, he slowly lifted her hand to his lips and kissed each fingertip.

Her breath hitched and came faster, and his sense of himself as a man, a man who could have an effect on a woman, swelled inside him, almost making him giddy.

This was Gabby, and the truth burst inside him: he'd never gotten over her, never stopped wishing they could be together, that they could make that family they'd dreamed of as kids. That was why he'd gotten so angry when she'd strayed: because the dream she'd shattered had been so big, so bright and shining.

In the back of his mind, a voice of caution scolded and warned. She'd gone out with his cousin. She'd had a child with another man. What had been so major in his emotional life hadn't been so big in hers.

He shouldn't trust her. And he definitely shouldn't kiss her.

But when had he ever done what he should? He nipped at her finger, soothed it with a kiss and then lowered his lips to hers.

Chapter Seven

⟜❧⟞

The feel of Reese's lips on hers was like coming home. Gabby sighed and nestled closer.

He was quick to gather her in and deepen the kiss, and coming home became a whole lot more exciting and intense.

She could smell his aftershave, the same faint, spicy scent he'd worn when they'd known each other in high school. She inhaled it as if it were air, necessary oxygen. Her face and neck felt hot, and her insides caught fire.

They'd kissed like this before, only once, shortly before Reese had left for the service. Now they'd already escalated to that same intense level. That was dangerous. They weren't kids anymore; they were a man and a woman who were very, very attracted to each other.

She should back up and stop, and she would…in just a moment. First, she needed to feel the strength of his arms, run a finger over the stubble on his cheek.

"I'm sorry," he said, his voice deep and rough, a little dangerous. "I didn't think this would be happening. I'd have shaved."

"It's okay." She stood on tiptoe to kiss his lips once more. And then, as if by mutual agreement, they each took a step back.

"I don't want to stop." His eyes burned on her.

"Me, either," she admitted, "but we have to."

He nodded and took another step back. "Last time that happened, we didn't have to stop ourselves, because Brock walked in on us."

His words were a bucket of cold water, chilling her warm feelings. She stared unseeingly at him while a movie of bad memories played across her mind's screen.

Brock's full, sulky lips twisting into a pout as he saw them kissing. His pressure on her later: *you kissed him, now kiss me.*

And when she'd refused, he'd been offended and angry—an overindulged football star who'd never heard the word *no.*

That was when everything had spun out of control.

That was when…she squeezed her eyes shut and shook away the rest of the memories.

She'd already remembered enough: that she wasn't a naive girl anymore, but a woman with responsibilities, a mother.

"You should go." She pressed her hand to her mouth to keep more words from coming out. Reese could never learn what had happened. She'd made a decision to protect Brock's parents.

And on a less elevated level, she was terrified to see Reese's skeptical face, his eyes that were sure to doubt her story. She took another step back.

He looked surprised, a little hurt. "I'm sorry," he

said, reaching a hand out to her. "I thought…you're pretty irresistible."

If he didn't leave she'd blurt out the truth. And that, she'd resolved not to do. "Just, please, go," she said.

He nodded. "I'm sorry. We'll talk tomorrow, okay? After we've both cooled down."

"Sure." She was backing away fast now, until she bumped into the couch and sat down abruptly. She wrapped her arms around her middle and didn't look up again. Holding herself together.

Only when she heard the door click shut did she let her feelings and memories press her back into the couch cushions, nearly crushing her.

The next morning, Reese was full of restless energy even though he hadn't slept much the night before.

He'd been reliving that kiss and thinking about Gabby's reaction to it.

He walked into the barn half an hour before the boys would start arriving and did his usual check of the dogs and area. The smell of hay and the dogs' excited barking brought him back to earth.

He had his priorities: the boys and the dogs.

But there's more to a man than his work.

Last night, he'd gotten a glimpse of what it might be like to have a family, a home.

A warm, beautiful, loving wife.

He wanted all that with an intensity he hadn't known he could still feel. He'd lost his spark after Gabby's betrayal and the grimness of war and the difficulty of losing his hand. Even getting back to where he could be excited about his work had been a big accomplishment, and it had seemed like enough for him.

Now that Gabby had returned, seemed to feel something for him, shared a sweet, intense kiss…yeah. He wanted more. He wanted all of that.

Behind him, the barn door creaked and he turned to see Gabby come in, backlit by the rosy sky of sunrise, Biff trotting beside her. She wore the same gray hat she'd pulled down over her curls in high school. Her cheeks were pink, and her breath made clouds in the cold air.

She was lovely, and he smiled and walked toward her.

"Hey, Reese," she said as if it were any old day. She veered away from him, put Biff into his pen and then headed for the office. She put down her things and spun back out before he could join her there.

This definitely felt awkward.

"So, are our plans in place for the day? This is when we introduce the animals into the performance, right? What can I do to help it all go smoothly?"

Her questions and comments were apt, but he knew Gabby pretty well. She was talking to cover her nerves.

"About last night," he began.

Her face closed.

"Do you want to talk about it?" he asked. Now that he was closer to her, he could see that there were dark circles beneath her eyes, eyes that looked swollen. "Hey, whatever you're feeling, it's okay, and we can figure it out."

"It's not—" she began, and then the door creaked open again. This time it was the dog trainer, Hannah.

She was a good woman and a good friend, pretty in a no-nonsense kind of way, skilled at working with all kinds of dogs. Normally, he'd have been glad to see her, but she'd arrived at exactly the wrong time.

He'd barely had the time to introduce the two women when car doors slammed outside, indicating the arrival of the first of the boys. The conversation with Gabby would have to wait. "We'll talk later," he said into her ear.

She didn't nod. Just turned to greet the boys and help them get their coats and hats where they belonged instead of piled up in a heap on the floor.

His cell phone buzzed, and he checked it. A text from Paige. Can't come today.

Too bad, but that meant that his aunt wouldn't come, either, and that was a welcome relief. Especially when things between him and Gabby were feeling so awkward.

"Look," Gabby said to him and Hannah, "I'll work with the boys, have them practice their parts. That'll give you a chance to assess the animals and figure out what we can do with them." Without waiting for an answer, she hurried back over to greet the next group of arriving boys, including Jacob, who walked in rubbing his eyes.

It made all the sense in the world to divide the labor as she'd suggested. So why did he have the distinct feeling that she was running away?

"Okay, let's get to it." Hannah walked toward the dogs' pens, then glanced back over her shoulder at him. "You coming?"

"Yeah, sure." He followed as she moved slowly down the row of pens. He'd stop thinking about Gabby now, focus on the show, the boys, the dogs.

"So, you want the dogs to be part of the nativity scene. Dressed up as stable animals."

"Right. Well, I don't love the idea, but that's what the boys all want."

She pointed at a couple of medium-sized white dogs, both fairly docile. "They kind of look like sheep," she said doubtfully.

"I guess. Any tips on making them *act* like sheep?"

Hannah talked him through reinforcing their sit-stay behavior and then assigning each a shepherd armed with ample treat bags.

"How about Biff?" He indicated the big black dog. "One of our new boys, Jacob, has been working with him a lot. He's more teachable than I expected, although I wouldn't call him a fast learner."

"He's big as an ox," Hannah said, laughing as she knelt in front of the big dog's pen. "But could he play one? C'mere, boy." She opened the pen and brought Biff out, and Reese showed her the simple commands Jacob had taught the dog. All was fine until one of the other dogs started barking. Biff joined in enthusiastically and lunged toward the other dog's pen, practically pulling petite Hannah off her feet.

"Whoa!" She spoke a couple of quick, low commands, and Biff seemed to recognize the voice of authority; that, and a few of Hannah's dried chicken treats, got him back under control.

"If you want to use him," she said, "you probably need to have him anchored to something stable. And near an exit, in case he needs to be taken out. He's gentle enough, but if he got loose, he could scare people."

"Right," Reese said, distracted by the sound of Gabby's laughter, apparently about something one of the boys had said. It was wholehearted laughter, not repressed or hidden like that of some women. Winter sunlight glinted off her hair.

"Earth to Reese." Hannah sounded amused. "How's the rekindled romance going, anyway?"

He looked at her blankly and then processed what she'd said, and his face heated. "There's no rekindled romance. Or…" He broke off.

Hannah's eyes were steady on him, honest. They'd been friends for a lot of years, because she lived just down the street from his aunt and uncle, and she'd been nice when he'd first moved to town, surly and miserable.

He lifted his hands, palms up. "What can I say? I… There's interest."

"On your side, or on hers, or both?" She wasn't looking at him now. She'd moved on to the next pen and was clucking her tongue at Bundi, a small black poodle mix.

"On mine, for sure," he admitted. "I'm not certain how she feels about me."

"Have you talked to her?"

Reese frowned. Had they talked? They'd talked about a lot of things, and they'd kissed, but they hadn't really addressed the relationship, where it could go.

"It'd be worth trying that," she suggested as she gently encouraged the small black dog to come out of the pen.

"You're right. But—" He broke off. He'd been about to ask something too personal.

"But what? Hey, sweetie, come on, it's okay," she added to the dog.

"How does a woman feel about a man who isn't…

whole?" He waved his good hand at his empty sleeve. He'd gotten frustrated with his prosthesis and wasn't wearing it today.

She turned slowly to face him. "Are you kidding? You're the same as you always were, but now you're a hero. It's no problem."

"Not even…romantically?"

She dipped her chin and raised her eyebrows, studying him steadily. "Even romantically. You're no less of a man, Reese. And don't get a big head, but you're kinda good looking."

It was an embarrassing conversation, about as personal as you could get. But he'd needed to ask a woman, and Hannah was perfect—kind and matter-of-fact, not a gossip.

Still, it was awkward. Sweat dripped down the back of his neck despite the cold day. He really needed to change the subject. "Thanks. Now let's talk about Bundi."

The noise level had risen in the barn. Apparently, the boys were taking a break, and Wolf ambled over. "Do you think she can do the show?" he asked, kneeling to rub Bundi's ears.

Her stub of a tail wagged, her ears perking up at the sound of Wolf's voice.

"She sure likes you," Hannah said to Wolf.

"She's my project," the boy said. "Aren't you, girl?" He scooped her into his lap and she rolled onto her back for a belly rub.

"She has some dementia," Reese said. "I don't want to stress her out."

"Like my grandma," Wolf said matter-of-factly.

"But she still likes to be included in things, don't you, girl?"

Bundi stared adoringly up at him through cloudy eyes.

Hannah smiled. "You know how a lot of nativity scenes have a shepherd carrying a sheep around his shoulders? That might be a good type of role for her to play."

Wolf nodded. "Cool. I think I'm gonna be a shepherd, anyway, because I'm too big for any of the other costumes they borrowed. For a shepherd, all we need is a big old white sheet."

"Sounds like a plan." Hannah showed Wolf a few things he could do to stimulate Bundi's thinking and then called a couple of other boys over to help them work with the dogs who'd be used in the show. Pretty soon, all the boys were gathered around Hannah.

Gabby was cleaning up from their morning activities. It might be his only chance to talk to her.

And after conversing with Hannah, he knew that talking to Gabby was the right thing to do. Before any more kissing, there needed to be some serious talking. Especially considering how quickly the connection between them had ignited with just that one kiss.

"Hey, Gabby," he said. "Talk a couple of minutes in the office?"

She sucked in a breath and let it out in a sigh. "Look, Reese, I don't want to be unkind," she said, and broke off.

That didn't sound promising. "But…" he prompted.

"But I just don't think we should…you know…"

He was pretty sure he did know, but he needed for her to say it. So he waited.

"I just don't think we should start up again," she said, all in a rush.

"Can I ask why?" He pushed the words out past the sinking feeling in his gut.

She looked at the floor, shaking her head. "I have my reasons."

Disappointment settled over him like a dark cloud. Rejection just plain stunk.

He wondered whether Hannah had been wrong, whether it was because Gabby didn't want to be around a man with a disability. Somehow, that was better than thinking she just plain didn't like him. "Okay," he said, because what else could he say.

"Sorry," she said in a timid, mousy way that wasn't like her at all. Then she turned and scuttled over to where the boys and Hannah were working with the dogs.

Reese went the rest of the way into his office and sat on the edge of the desk. He *felt* like putting a fist through the wall. But when you had only one arm, you couldn't indulge in stuff like that, because losing use of your good hand, even for a little while, wasn't an option.

And anyway, he wasn't an angry kid anymore. He had more mature ways to work out his frustrations. He'd hit the gym after work, make it to the basketball game he'd been missing most weeks. Maybe stop for a run before or after. Cold weather notwithstanding, he had some energy to work off.

That would take care of the physical side. His heartache...now, that was another issue.

Gabby walked into Nana's house Friday night hoping for a quiet evening to cuddle her daughter and rest.

To shut out what had just happened with Reese, the puzzled, hurt look on his face.

Jacob was behind her, running a zigzag pattern with Biff, throwing a stick for him to fetch. She'd fix him and Nana an easy dinner and then disappear into her room with Izzy.

But when she walked inside, the smell of Nana's homemade lasagna filled the air. Christmas music played, and Izzy sat in her high chair, banging a spoon on the tray and grinning.

Nana stood at the counter tossing a salad, wearing the same apron she'd always worn, and the sight of her looking so strong and healthy made tears sting Gabby's eyes.

"Ma-ma!" Izzy threw the spoon to the floor and held up her arms.

Gabby shrugged out of her coat, dropped her things and hurried over to sweep Izzy out of her high chair and give her a kiss. Then she went to Nana and put an arm around her. "This smells amazing! You must be feeling better?"

"I got a burst of energy, and at my age, it's use it or lose it." She patted Gabby's arm. "Wash up and call Jacob, and we'll sit down and eat." She opened the oven door and peered inside, and Gabby caught a whiff of fresh, buttery garlic bread. Her stomach growled. "We'll be right back, won't we, sweetie?" She bounced Izzy, making her laugh. Then she went to the door. "Jacob, come in for dinner! Nana made lasagna and you don't want to miss it!"

An hour later, they'd all eaten their fill, and Jacob and Gabby were finishing up the dishes while Nana held Izzy. Her energy was clearly fading, but she was all smiles.

"You know what would top off that dinner?" she asked. "Cookies. Why don't you two make us some Christmas cookies?"

Gabby's heart sank. She'd rallied and enjoyed the dinner, but she was exhausted.

Looking from Nana's bright eyes to Jacob's matching ones, though, she couldn't say no.

"What kind of Christmas cookies do you like best, Jacob?" Nana asked.

His mouth twisted to one side as he thought. "Hmm...maybe those little round white ones."

Gabby looked at Nana. "Snowballs? With powdered sugar that gets all over?"

"Yeah, those!" Jacob looked from one of them to the other. "Could we really make them?"

Gabby went to the refrigerator and cupboard. "Looks like we have everything." She got out the ingredients, wondering about something, and not sure she should ask. But the question burst out of her: "Did Mom make these for you?"

Because she'd certainly never made them for Gabby.

She'd rarely talked to Jacob about their mother. He didn't volunteer much, and Gabby was still a little tender about the fact that their mother had raised Jacob but not her.

"Are you kidding?" Jacob snorted. "She never baked any cookies. She never cooked anything."

"What did you eat, dear?" Nana sounded upset, and Gabby knew why. She'd raised her daughter to be a good person, but the drugs had made her a stranger.

"Fast food," he said. "Or stuff from the neighbors,

or the soup kitchen. I don't think she knew how to cook." He looked at Gabby. "Did she ever cook for you?"

"Not that I remember." And this was getting sad. "Thankfully, Nana taught me a few things about cooking once I came to live with her. We've had some cookie-baking marathons in our day." She bent and put her arms around her grandmother from the back, giving her a quick hug.

"I never did anything like this before." Jacob waved a hand around the kitchen, and Gabby knew what he meant. The cooking, the eating together, the easy conversations, all of it was new to him. And suddenly, that last little bit of resentment she'd felt toward Jacob faded away. Their mother had done Gabby a favor, leaving her for Nana to raise, because Nana had created a real home for her.

The least she could do was help make the same thing happen for Jacob. As he followed her directions about creaming butter and sugar together, his cowlick sticking up, concentrating on his work, Gabby felt a huge rush of love for him.

She'd been thinking about making this Christmas good for Izzy, since it was her first one. But Jacob was actually the more deprived.

While the cookies baked, Jacob held Izzy, bouncing her and making her laugh, being just a little rougher than Gabby normally was with her. When Gabby started to caution him, though, Nana put a finger to her lips. "That's what men do for babies," she said. "They teach them about where their bodies are in space, teach them to accept rougher play. Let him interact with his niece his own way."

After the cookies came out and cooled enough for Jacob to wolf down six or seven of them, he muttered something about video games and headed for his room. "You go to bed, too," Gabby said to Nana, who looked tired. "I'll clean up after I get Izzy to sleep."

Izzy fell to sleep almost instantly, and when Gabby came back to the kitchen, Nana was still sitting in her chair at the table.

"Sit down a minute," Nana said. "The rest of the cleanup can wait until morning."

Gabby sat at the table and studied Nana with concern, hoping her conversation with Jacob about their mother hadn't upset her. "Is everything okay?"

"That's exactly what I wanted to ask you," Nana said.

"Ask me? Why?"

Nana reached out and took Gabby's hand between her two soft, papery ones. "You've seemed tense, or blue, for the past couple of days. Has something happened?"

Gabby looked into those knowing eyes that had seen through every teenage half-truth she'd tried to pull off. "Sort of," she said, "but I… I don't think I'm ready to talk about it."

"Is it Reese?"

"You see too much." Gabby stood, restless, and got plastic wrap to put over the plate of snowball cookies.

"You know, dear," Nana said, "I'll always listen when you're ready to talk about Izzy's father and what happened."

Gabby froze in the act of closing the box of plastic wrap. She looked up to find her grandmother's eyes on her, observant, piercing.

"You never talked about it at the time," Nana went on. "I barely knew you were pregnant, when suddenly I had a great-granddaughter."

That was because Gabby had deliberately stayed away.

"I'll tell you someday, probably," she said, "but now isn't the time."

"Just answer me one question," Nana said. "Is Reese Izzy's father?"

Gabby stared at her and then bit her lip. "No," she said. "No, he's not."

Nana nodded. "I didn't think so. If there were a chance of that, Reese is the type of man that would find out and take care of you."

Nana was right. Reese kept his promises and followed up on his responsibilities. That was who he was.

But what would Reese—or Nana, or anyone—think if they ever discovered the truth? Would anyone believe she'd not consented to being with Brock, when he was so popular, so wealthy, so handsome?

Once again his words came back to her. *"Don't try telling anyone you didn't want this. No one will believe a nothing like you."* The words had burned through her anguish about the assault, because they'd had the ring of truth.

No one in town would believe her.

Maybe, possibly, Nana might...but Gabby couldn't face the possibility that she wouldn't.

And Reese? No. He'd had a rivalry with his cousin even back then, and there was no way he'd believe her now.

And watching him condemn her for something that truly hadn't been her fault, something that had been the worst thing to ever happen to her…she just wasn't strong enough to face that.

"Keeping secrets inside can be toxic," Nana said earnestly. "I'm not saying you have to talk to me about it, but I hope you'll talk to someone. If Izzy's father is living, she deserves to know him. Unless there's a reason she shouldn't." Again with the piercing blue gaze.

It was almost as if Nana knew, or guessed, that Izzy's conception hadn't been consensual.

"I've talked about it," she said, which was true. She'd talked to a counselor at the college, extensively, enough to work through her guilt and believe it wasn't her fault.

But with Brock dead—and idolized—there was no one to be angry at, no one to blame. "Thank you for caring so much," she said, standing and kissing Nana's cheek. "I think we should both get some rest." She paused, then added, "Thank you for making such a wonderful home for me."

"You're the light of my life," Nana said simply. "You, and now Izzy."

That brought tears to Gabby's eyes. As she helped Nana up, she shot a prayer of thanks heavenward. Out of sorrow, joy. It was God's way, wrenching and beautiful.

Chapter Eight

The next day, Saturday, Reese had to dig a path from the road to the barn. Six inches of heavy snow had fallen during the night. Now snow-lined branches pointed toward a cloudy sky that promised to yield more of the white stuff soon.

The impending bad weather matched Reese's mood. And it *wasn't* just about Gabby; it was about the future of the Rescue Haven program. What if they couldn't show their effectiveness to Mr. Romano? What if the program died for a lack of funding?

It was pure folly to depend so heavily on one donor, and if Reese had time, he'd be out pounding on doors trying to drum up more support. There was a stack of grant applications on his desk that needed filling out, a complicated process. And there were reports to be written so that they didn't lose the minimal funding they already had.

But he didn't have time to work on any of that, because he had to shovel snow and organize the boys to do a performance that seemed destined to be a disaster.

He'd barely gotten the path shoveled clear when parents started dropping boys off, most of them stressed and complaining about their icy commute to work.

The boys' moods seemed as gloomy as the weather. Gloomy as their parents' and Reese's moods, or maybe he was just projecting. But no, he thought as he listened to their complaints. They were really cranky today.

"I ain't working on that show *again*." That was Wolf. And when the biggest and oldest and most influential kid complained, the others were bound to follow suit.

"This is getting to be like school," David said. Reese could have been glad the two of them agreed on something, but unfortunately, it was something negative.

"It's my vacation," said Connor, "and I coulda stayed home in bed, but my mom said I had to come *here*."

The negative attitudes seemed to be as contagious as a bad epidemic of flu, and they shook Reese out of his worries about the financing of the program. He wanted to save the Rescue Haven program, desperately wanted it. But what was the use if the program was a drag and no boys wanted to come?

He was tempted to just declare a free, fun day. But the show needed work, and a lot of it; it just wasn't very good. Not only that, but these particular boys didn't do well with unstructured time.

He rubbed the back of his neck and looked upward, hoping God or his memory would supply him with a good idea. And something came to him. When he'd been doing carpentry and hit a rough patch, rather than pounding the work out anyway, he'd go off into nature. A few hours of hiking or chopping wood for the local farmers had usually given him the inspiration he needed.

The boys needed inspiration for the show, and here they were in the middle of a beautiful, snowy place. There had to be a way to get them outdoors and active. At a minimum, it would cheer them up; ideally, it would also spark some ideas in them to improve the show they were working on.

There was a hearty, feminine laugh he would have recognized anywhere. While he'd been ruminating, Gabby had apparently come in. The boys were groaning to her, and she was teasing with them, laughing her sparkling laugh, cheering them up.

Watching her made all his feelings rush back. He'd gotten full of foolish hope, kissing her. He wanted to do that again. A lot.

But although she'd seemed to like it just fine at the time, almost immediately she'd thought better of it. He could think of plenty of reasons he wasn't good enough, but knowing that didn't soothe the ache in his heart.

He sucked in a breath and pushed those thoughts away as he beckoned her over. "I know you were planning to teach them to sew today, work on costumes, but I'm not sure they can sit still for it this morning."

"We need to get the costumes done." She bit her lip and looked at the boys roughhousing and arguing. "But I see what you mean. You know them best. If you have another idea of what to do with them today, go for it, and I'll tag along and help."

He liked that about Gabby. She wasn't bossy, insistent on getting her own way. She could listen and be flexible. It reminded him of how she'd been when they'd been in school together, and that gave him a brainstorm. "I'd like to take them sledding," he said.

Her face lit up. "They'd love that. Where?"

Then they looked at each other, and Reese was pretty sure they were having the same idea at the same time.

"Romano's Mountain," she said slowly.

He nodded. "It's still the best place around."

Their eyes met again, just for a few seconds, and then they both looked away. Too much remembering. They'd gone sledding at Romano's Mountain when they'd first started dating; it was where they'd shared their first quick, awkward kiss. Even now, he could remember the way she'd started to fall on a slippery patch of ice. He'd caught and steadied her, held on a little too long, and then, impulsively, leaned in and brushed his lips over hers.

Even then, young and inexperienced as they both were, it had been electric. They'd both pulled back quickly, stared at each other. He for one had known that moment that she was the girl for him.

At least, that was what he'd thought at the time, when he was young and romantic and idealistic. Full of happy dreams about how life could be.

He'd been wrong, of course. Because even after their much more intense kiss a couple of days ago, she'd told him in no uncertain terms that she wasn't interested in a relationship.

So much for romantic, happy dreams.

The boys were sounding rowdier now, getting out of control, and he pushed away his own memories to focus on today. "The problem is, Romano will never let us sled there," he said. "He's not exactly a fan of our group, our boys."

"It's such a good idea, though." Gabby frowned for a moment and then snapped her fingers. "Why don't we offer to shovel all his walks and that huge driveway of his? Maybe it's a better idea to connect with him than avoid him."

"That'll take a lot of shoveling," he said. "But...you might be right. Better to try to win him over a little bit now, instead of putting all our eggs into that one basket of the show."

She wrinkled her nose. "Exactly. That might not have been my brightest idea."

"Do you think?" He softened his words with a smile, because something about today made him not want to argue with her.

She nodded over at the roughhousing boys. "They have a lot of energy. We can borrow shovels from Nana, and the church."

"And Uncle Clive's snowblower. They'll love that."

"Let's do it." She smiled at him, bright and sunny, and he was the same kind of bowled over he'd been as a teen.

Or almost the same. The difference was that now, he didn't have the simple optimism he'd had then, the same faith that things could work out between them.

Gabby loved the idea of sledding Romano's Mountain, except for the dangerous memories the place evoked.

They borrowed shovels and sleds, and the boys expended a ton of energy: first shoveling Mr. Romano's long driveway with more speed than finesse, and then running up and sliding down Romano's Mountain—really more of a hill, but it counted for a mountain in Ohio—in the cold air. Their moods brightened, even more when Gabby got reluctant permission for them to build a fire in the old fire barrel at the bottom of Romano's Mountain.

While the boys gathered wood and built the fire, Gabby drove to the store and bought hot dogs and buns. Some of these boys had never eaten hot dogs cooked over an open fire—just like she hadn't, not until she'd been a teenager visiting friends—and she wanted to give them the opportunity. She threw in a bag of marshmallows, too, and a day that had started out dreary suddenly became festive.

Reese was showing the boys how to keep the fire going when she returned, and soon they all had full stomachs. They needed to get to the church for their afternoon rehearsal, but it was hard to leave the warmth and camaraderie of the fire.

When Reese used his prosthesis to help with the cleanup, one of the younger boys blurted out, "How does that work?"

"Shut up!" another boy whispered.

"How does it even stay on?"

Reese looked around at the circle of curious boys, and Gabby's heart went out to him. It had to be hard enough to deal with the physical challenges of learning to live with one arm, but the emotional challenge of having people want to talk about it might be almost as bad. "Guys," she said, "maybe Reese doesn't want to talk about it, and that's his choice."

"It's fine." Reese shrugged, and it seemed to Gabby that he purposely held his prosthetic hook in the air an extra moment so the boys could get a good look. "I'd rather have you ask questions than just stare or talk among yourselves. Do you want to see how it works?"

All of the boys nodded or smiled or both.

He knelt close to the fire and slipped off his jacket and then his flannel shirt. In his white T-shirt, he looked like a bodybuilder, and Gabby sucked in a breath, her face heating. *Wow.*

He showed them how the prosthetic arm had straps fitted around his back and how he used tension to make the hand move. He reached for a stick and picked it up and handed it to David. Then he fumbled with another one. "I'm still learning how to make it work right," he said. "Some guys can pick up a marble and shoot it, but I'm not there yet."

"Can you take it off?" one of the boys asked.

"Yeah!"

"Hmm." A faint flush climbed up Reese's face. "Some of you might not want to see it." He didn't look at Gabby.

"Oh, c'mon. We all want to see it, right?"

"Is it gross?"

"Miss Gabby might not," Wolf said.

"Oh, yeah." All those disappointed faces turned her way.

She studied Reese's face and didn't see reluctance there. "I've got to admit, I'm curious," she said, "but it's up to you, Reese."

He shrugged and unstrapped the prosthesis, slid it off and offered it to the boys to examine.

"How come you've got that?" David pointed at the sock-like piece of cloth that covered what remained of Reese's arm.

"Helps the prosthesis fit better. Soaks up perspiration." He leaned closer. "And it's really not gross under there. It's just scar tissue. Like you have under your chin, where you cut yourself."

"This is so cool!" one of the boys said, making the prosthetic claw open and close. "I wouldn't mind having one of these."

"Yes, you would," Reese said, taking the prosthesis back and strapping it on. "It's tough to deal with at times. I'm right-handed, so I've had to learn to do a lot of things all over again, like handwriting and throwing a ball. And the fit isn't perfect, so sometimes I have to take a break from wearing it."

"Plus, it looks weird," one of the younger boys said. "Some girls might not want to go out with you."

All eyes turned to Reese at that declaration.

Reese sucked in a breath. "You could be right."

Gabby couldn't let that go. "Most women would be glad to go out with a man who's served his country," she said firmly.

"But it's kinda weird, isn't it?" Conner asked.

"Not to me," she said, "and not to any woman worth having. Anyway, it's what's inside that counts, and all of you should keep that in mind when you start dating."

She didn't look at Reese at all while speaking her mind, but she hoped he was listening. Mostly he seemed self-confident, but the fact remained that he'd had a major physical change, and that had to be tough.

"Gabby's not like other women," Jacob said, a note of pride in his voice.

"You're right," Reese said. "She's not." He flashed

her a smile as he shrugged back into his jacket. "Okay, everyone, let's head back to the barn and gather our stuff. We have a show to put on."

It took two van trips to get all the boys and dogs hauled over to the church that afternoon, and even then Gabby had to drive separately, bringing Nana and Izzy. Nana was going to help with the sewing, and Izzy, as usual, was cheerfully along for the ride.

Being around all the boys in the Rescue Haven program was good for Izzy. Between them, and Reese and Jacob, she'd gotten used to deeper voices and a slightly rougher style of interaction, and as a result, she was more confident and happier than ever. Since Gabby didn't expect to raise her with a father in the home, all the boys and men surrounding her now were a godsend.

As they got out of the van, she heard a few of the boys complaining. They were tired. They were cold. They didn't want to hang out in a church.

But it was good-natured complaining, not like the slightly hostile tone they'd had this morning. Reese had called it right, getting them all outdoors for fresh air and exercise.

Reese called a lot of stuff right. He was good at his job, and if she hadn't known him before, she'd never have guessed that working with kids wasn't his first choice of career.

God worked in mysterious ways. Reese had been truly gifted at carpentry, but wasn't he affecting even more boys, for the better, in his current position? Just look at how he'd gently educated the boys about his prosthesis, modeling gracious acceptance of a disability and calm, secure leadership.

Nana squeezed her arm as they walked together up the icy sidewalk. "I'm so proud of you for how you've embraced this work," she said. "You've grown into an impressive woman."

Her words warmed Gabby, and so did the voice behind them. "I'll second that," a familiar voice said.

"Sheniqua!" Gabby spun around and hugged her old friend. "It's great to see you, but what are you doing at the church today?"

"Even doctors get a little time off," Sheniqua said. "And you know I like quilting and sewing, so when your grandma said you all were working with the boys here at the church today…I thought I'd stop by, see if I could help." She held up a plastic container and flipped open the lid. "Plus, I brought cookies."

Drawn by the delicious fragrance, several boys circled them.

Gabby inhaled with deep appreciation. "Chocolate chip. You're the absolute best," she said.

"Could I try one?" David asked.

Wolf elbowed him out of the way. "I can help you carry that, ma'am."

Sheniqua held the container out of reach. "Wait your turn, boys. Nana and Gabby—and Reese, where is he?—anyway, the adults get the first pick before I give the rest to you young people."

Nana and Gabby quickly took warm cookies and Gabby took an extra one for Reese, wrapping it in a napkin. Then Sheniqua handed the container to Wolf and told him to distribute the cookies fairly.

As Sheniqua, Nana and Gabby walked into the

church, Sheniqua put an arm around Gabby. "Your grandma's right, you know? You're all grown up now. I remember you in middle school, and oh boy! I'd never have guessed you'd turn into this mature, cool, together woman at, what, twenty-three?"

"I'm together?" But even as she snorted, Gabby's mind turned over the words. Maybe she *was* getting it together, at least a little bit. "Thanks. You were always so cool yourself. I never thought I'd come to see you as a friend I could actually hang out and relax with, but I do." They hadn't seen much of each other since Gabby's middle school years, because Gabby had spent so little time in town, and Sheniqua, as a med student and then a physician, was insanely busy. But they'd talked on the phone a few times each year. First, it had been Sheniqua checking in with a younger girl as an act of service, and then later, when she'd become Nana's doctor, about Nana's health. All along, she and Gabby had felt close enough to discuss a little bit about their personal lives. When Gabby had come home for Christmas, she'd called Sheniqua and conversation had flowed between them as equals. They'd made plans for a coffee date over the weekend.

Gabby was grateful to be renewing old friendships. It was starting to feel like she was building a life here in Bethlehem Springs.

As she unloaded sewing supplies from a couple of boxes, Gabby thought more about what Nana and Sheniqua had said. She *was* more mature and more together than she'd ever expected to be. Motherhood had a way of making you grow up fast.

She felt stronger now, less scared. It crossed her mind that if the assault had happened to her now, if something like that ever happened again, she'd roar like a tigress. She might not be able to stop it from happening, but she'd never keep silent.

She had to have compassion on her younger self for covering it up and running away. But in the face of her grandmother's and Sheniqua's supportive words, something occurred to her: maybe, just maybe, she didn't need to do it anymore. Why should she take on the responsibility for keeping the Markowskis in the dark about their son's criminal act? And if there were people who didn't believe her, well, so what? She knew what had happened. Talking about it wasn't a crime, and anyone who knew and loved her would take her word for it. As for the gossips…well, they'd think what they wanted to think, anyway, no matter what she said.

Obviously, she needed to think about it and pray about it before taking steps to reveal what had happened to her. Figure out whether there was a way to reveal the truth to a few key people, close friends and family, without causing pain to Brock's parents.

But now wasn't the time to figure all that out; she had responsibilities.

"Okay, guys," she said, clapping her hands to get the attention of the boys who were milling around. "I need three people over here to cut fabric. Once we have the pieces for the shepherd costumes, we'll go to work cutting out the animal ones."

"And I'm going to show the rest of you how to sew," Nana said. "If you've already learned, you can help someone next to you. Let's start with a running stitch." She waved strips of colorful cloth around like flags, drawing the attention of several boys.

Gabby had a moment of worry that the boys

wouldn't want to spend time with an older lady like Nana. But several actually seemed eager to sit beside her. Something she said made them laugh, and a couple of other boys joined her circle.

That was Nana: charismatic to people of all ages. And these boys, many of whom had had instability in their home lives, seemed to gravitate to Nana with her warmth and groundedness.

Gabby's heart swelled with love for the woman who'd selflessly taken her in and raised her without once making her feel like she wasn't wanted and loved. Now that Gabby was a mother herself, she had an inkling of the sacrifice involved.

Reese, Jacob and Wolf came in with the dogs. The two white ones were barking a little, and Gabby bit her lip, wondering if their group would bother the pastor in his study or the groups meeting elsewhere in the church. But they quieted down quickly. Biff, to her amazement, walked beside Jacob in a decent heel position, and Wolf held Bundi in his arms.

She'd just gotten her group of boys started cutting fabric from a simple pattern when the door opened with a bang, and Mr. Romano walked in.

"He always did have to make an entrance," Nana muttered. "Are you here to thank the boys for shoveling, Santiago?" she called to him in a louder voice.

He raised an eyebrow at her, but when the boys all looked expectantly in his direction, he waved a hand. "Much appreciated, boys," he said. "You did quick work."

A chorus of "you're welcome" and "no problem" came from the boys.

He walked around overlooking the scene, and Gabby sidled over to Reese, standing off in a corner of the room. "What's he doing here?" she asked, feeling uneasy.

Reese shrugged. "He's a member of the church board, so I suppose he's just checking on what happens in the church. I don't think he really came to thank the boys in person, but your grandmother forced him into it."

"Nana and Mr. Romano have known each other for probably eighty years, and fought for most of it," she said.

The dogs barked when Mr. Romano walked by, and he did a double take. He muttered something about rules and animals in the church, but Sheniqua, whom Gabby had updated on the Rescue Haven situation, walked over and distracted him by showing him the costumes she and Nana were helping the boys to make.

"We'd better go make nice," Reese said.

"I guess we should talk to him," Gabby said at the same moment.

They met each other's eyes, and that special spark they'd always had arced between them. It was hard to look away, and when she finally did, Gabby felt a little bit out of breath.

Keeping herself out of a relationship with Reese was proving harder than she'd ever expected.

Maybe you don't need to.

The idea wouldn't leave her alone. Nana was unfailing in her compassion, and Reese...the warm way he looked at her and spoke with her gave her hope that, now that they'd reconnected, he'd be supportive, as well.

She definitely needed to pray about it. But the possibility of coming out of hiding gave her a giddy feeling.

They reached Mr. Romano as he approached the group of boys Nana was overseeing. "Boys, sewing?" he asked skeptically.

"Is there a problem with that?" Nana gave him a challenging stare.

He lifted his hands, palms out. "No, no problem." He looked up, noticed Gabby and Reese and frowned at them. "Those boys didn't do an especially good job on my driveway, you know."

Behind them, a chair screeched out and Nana stood so quickly she had to grab the back of the chair for balance. "Were you ever young?" she asked him.

He threw up his hands. "I'm just letting them know that I expect a higher quality of work at the performance next week. And there's not much time."

"It'll be great, Mr. Romano," Gabby said, stepping between him and Nana. Really, they looked like they might come to blows. Reese came beside her, and she elbowed him. "Right, Reese?"

"Um, yes. We surely hope so."

Mr. Romano looked around the room, shook his head and strode toward the inner door. Probably to talk to the pastor about the wrong use they were making of the church.

She looked up at Reese. "I'm going to get working on the animal costumes. As soon as we have a decent set of outfits, we need to start rehearsing so the animals can get used to being where we'll actually do the show."

"Got it. Boys, too." He gave her a little smile as he headed toward a group that was studying the sound equipment.

David and another younger boy were grooming the

white dogs with brushes and combs. Gabby helped them tie bows in the dogs' hair, and they all decided they were a decent facsimile of Christmas lambs. Biff amicably let them put a pair of ox horns on him, and everything was fine until he saw a squirrel out the window and lunged for it. It took both Gabby and Jacob to restrain him, and she vowed anew to make sure he was tied to something on the night of the show.

Wolf was trying to brush Bundi, but all the activity around them had made her pant, her cloudy eyes going white around the edges. Wolf put the brush down, sat cross-legged and simply held the senior dog. "It's okay," he crooned. "You're fine the way you are. You look real pretty. I'll just carry you like this."

Bundi looked up at him with obvious adoration and settled into his lap.

Gabby bit her lip as tears sprung to her eyes. The big, tough teen nurturing the small, confused dog was exactly what the Rescue Haven program was all about.

From across the room, she heard Izzy wail and got to her feet. But before she was halfway there, Reese picked her up and held her tenderly, bouncing her a little and talking to her as he walked her around the room. Soon she was all smiles, and Gabby's heart melted a little more.

Look how sweet he's being with Izzy. He had a soft, understanding heart beneath all the manly bluster.

She wanted to tell him the truth about Izzy, she realized as she walked across the room. She *could* tell him. She was going to do it.

She reached him just as he lifted Izzy in the air, making her laugh. "Thanks for taking care of her," she said. "When you have time, we need to talk."

Chapter Nine

That night, Reese whistled as he walked into the elegant steakhouse on the outskirts of Cleveland.

Not that dining with his aunt and uncle was exactly what he wanted to be doing.

Although normally he'd be excited about the fine food he'd be eating, tonight he couldn't care less about that. He'd much rather be sharing some Crock-Pot stew with Gabby and her family, as she'd invited him to do.

But the great thing was, she'd invited him. And after the electricity in the air between them at the church today, he had a good feeling about that. They'd agreed to meet up tomorrow; that was what had him whistling.

"We need to talk," she'd said. What did she want to talk to him about?

He didn't dare get his hopes up too high, but it was undeniable that she'd been more than friendly today, that there had been a spark between them and that her request to talk with him had been warm, accompanied by a sweet smile.

He realized he had a foolish grin on his face and tried to pull himself back to the here and now. White tablecloths and clinking crystal glasses didn't make for his favorite environment. He'd just as soon go to a diner. But thanks to spending his teenage years in his aunt and uncle's house, he knew how to act in a place like this. He had them to thank for that.

He was feeling uncommonly grateful tonight, grateful for everything.

Maybe he'd bring Gabby here sometime, just for a kick; with her, it would be fun.

Just like a picnic or a pizza would be fun with her.

And when you started thinking that any activity you could name would be more fun with your special someone, well…it might be about time to make a move, see if she'd consider taking it to the next level. Dating, being exclusive, making a start at a commitment.

The thought made his insides spin.

"Reese, darling." His aunt waved, and his uncle stood, and he wove his way through the tables, hugged them both, then sat down.

"Where's your prosthesis, dear?" His aunt looked concerned.

"That's hardly a question to start a conversation," Uncle Clive scolded.

Reese waved away his uncle's concern. "It's fine. We're family." He turned to his aunt. "It's a process, getting used to it and getting the right fit. I was having some abrasions, and when that happens, the docs say to leave it off some."

"And you don't want to scare the boys by leaving it off around them," Uncle Clive said. "I understand that."

"Nor around Gabby Hanks," his aunt said, the slightest curl of her lip showing her attitude.

He thought of how open-minded the boys and Gabby had been earlier today. *They* didn't seem to be the ones scared off by looking at or thinking about his prosthesis. His aunt and uncle were a different story.

Oh, well. He found it didn't bother him much.

What did bother him was Aunt Catherine's attitude toward Gabby. Where it came from, he didn't know. His aunt was always snobbish, but he didn't remember her having anything in particular against Gabby when they'd both been in high school.

He shrugged. "I'm just wearing it on a schedule, like the docs suggested," he explained. "Most folks barely seem to notice one way or the other."

Which was a blessing. At first, he'd felt like everyone who saw him was staring at the place where his right hand should have been. But that had been his own discomfort and self-consciousness talking, not reality.

After a little chitchat, Uncle Clive cleared his throat. "Tell us about how your show for the church is going."

He looked over at Aunt Catherine. "You've seen the rehearsals, right?"

"Earlier this week," she said, "but I hope you're further along now."

"Today was a breakthrough," he said, and told them about the animals and costumes, the good rehearsal they'd had. "It's too bad Paige couldn't be there for today's rehearsal, but we're hoping she can come to the Saturday one, and again on Monday," he added. "She's a good influence on the boys."

"She'll be there," Uncle Clive promised. "And…we might even do a little more for your program. But we have a few questions first."

"Sure." He'd be shocked beyond words if they

wanted to donate, but he wouldn't turn their money away. Maybe Paige's involvement was a good thing in more ways than her considerable singing, acting and leadership abilities. "What do you want to know?"

Aunt Catherine leaned forward. "Tell us about your relationship with Gabby."

He blinked. "What does that have to do with the Rescue Haven program?"

"Potentially, quite a lot," his uncle said.

"I'm not sure how that could be. But for now, Gabby and I are friends." It was true he wanted to be more, but his aunt and uncle didn't need to know that.

His aunt tilted her head to one side. "I've seen what looks like…interest. Of a romantic kind."

She didn't say on whose side, and Reese wanted to ask her: *Really? Is Gabby interested in me?* But that smacked of the playground, and anyway, he didn't want his aunt involved in his love life. "As I said, we're friends. But I'm still not sure what that has to do with anything."

Aunt Catherine sighed. "We're just trying to save you from heartbreak, Reese."

Something was suspicious about her concern. She'd never much cared about his heart before. "I appreciate that," he said, "but I'm fine."

"Not if you fall in love with that…that *woman*," Uncle Clive said.

"We're just afraid she's not going to accept you." Aunt Catherine looked pointedly at his empty sleeve.

That stunned him into blurting it out: "You think she won't accept me because of my disability?"

"It could be a problem," Uncle Clive said.

"Women…you just don't have much experience with them," Aunt Catherine added.

He frowned, looking from one to another, his face feeling unaccountably hot. "Gabby's not like that," he said.

"We just hate to see you hurt," his aunt said.

"We'd like to see you doing something positive," Uncle Clive said. "And so…" He trailed off, looking at his wife. "We'd like to make a contribution to the Rescue Haven program."

"But only if you let Gabby Hanks go."

"What?" He stared at them as anger started to boil. "You mean *fire* her? For what?" He'd heard from his former assistant that she definitely wasn't coming back, and the more he worked with Gabby, the more he liked the idea of keeping her on, if she'd stay. The notion of firing her was plain ridiculous.

"Now, don't get upset." His uncle pursed his lips. "We've been talking, that's all, and we think it would be best. For the good of the program."

The waiter brought their meals then, and Reese stared blankly at his giant steak. "I didn't order this." And he wouldn't have, because how was he supposed to cut a steak with one hand?

"We knew what you always ordered," Aunt Catherine said. And then, as the waiter fussed around delivering the rest of the food and Reese just looked at his steak, she made a small, strained sound. "Clive," she said faintly, "he can't cut it."

Heat rose in Reese's neck and face. There was probably a way to do it one-handed; he looked up how-to videos almost every day and was learning all kinds of workarounds for his disability. But he'd never looked up cutting a steak; it hadn't been an issue before.

And it wasn't as if he could google it on his phone and figure it out, not here and not with his aunt and uncle staring at him.

Suddenly, he felt more nauseated than hungry.

"Hey, don't think a thing of it. I'll cut it." Uncle Clive pulled Reese's plate over and began slicing the steak up. "How's that, eh? Good size of bites?"

"It's fine." Reese wished the floor would open up and swallow him. Having his meat cut up for him like a toddler stabbed him right in the gut.

He took deep breaths and tried to remember what the therapists and social workers at the VA had said. Breathe through the uncomfortable situations. Keep your sense of humor. Most people don't mean to be insensitive; they're just awkward around differences. Don't focus on what you can't do.

Which meant Reese needed to stop focusing on his cut-up steak and figure out his aunt and uncle's agenda. They were definitely acting strange. He couldn't understand their animosity toward Gabby. "Just explain your thinking to me, on the Rescue Haven program and on Gabby," he said. "I don't get it."

His aunt took a delicate sip of water. "Back to our, er, potential donation. We know your program is at risk. And frankly, the chances of getting that group up to performance level by Monday night are pretty slim."

Uncle Clive pushed his plate of neatly cut steak bites back toward him. "If you don't get the go-ahead from that church board, you're going under. But we have a check right here that can pull you back out of the red."

"You could help hundreds of boys, Reese," his aunt said.

Reese forked up a bite of steak. "I don't understand why Gabby Hanks has anything to do with whether you'll donate."

"Eat your steak," Uncle Clive urged. "And just know that we have our reasons."

"Gabby was a bad influence on Brock." His aunt pushed lettuce leaves around her salad bowl. "You weren't here when that happened, but it soured us on her."

"We're just trying to do for you what we didn't do for Brock," his uncle said. "Dig in, dig in!" He took his steak knife and cut into his own rare steak.

Reese watched the red juices pool on the plate. "You're going to have to be a lot more specific than that," he said. "It's hard for me to imagine Gabby being any kind of a bad influence. She's a great person."

His aunt pressed her lips together and nodded. "That's what we thought, too."

"What changed your mind?"

"Just…a number of things." Uncle Clive gestured with his fork. "Eat up."

"It's just a feeling we had," his aunt added.

So Reese did eat, because he was hungry and the steak was good. But though he continued to probe about what might be behind his aunt and uncle's attitude, he didn't get any answers. He plowed through his steak and potato, even had dessert at their insistence, spoke with a couple of their acquaintances and listened to his aunt brag about his war record, smiled and nodded as the folks thanked him for his service.

His good mood had disappeared. His aunt and uncle

weren't people whose lifestyle he admired or shared, but they'd raised him after his parents had died. They must have good intentions at heart, right?

As they said their goodbyes, his uncle pulled him to the side. "I know you'll need time to think about this proposition," he said, "but we really would like to help out your program."

Reese narrowed his eyes. "But only if I'll fire Gabby."

"And avoid her socially, as well. For your own protection."

"She's become indispensable to Rescue Haven's daily activities," he said. Had that been a mistake?

"And to you?" Uncle Clive narrowed his eyes and studied Reese.

"We're friends," Reese repeated through gritted teeth.

"It wouldn't take much to get rid of her," Uncle Clive said. "I think if you turn a cold shoulder to her, she'll get the message. I suspect she's acting affectionate because she wants something out of you."

"She's not—"

"I know, you think she's not that kind of person. But we men tend to get a little shortsighted when there's an attractive woman acting overfriendly." He patted Reese's shoulder. "Just think about it."

Irritation surged through Reese's entire body as he said polite goodbyes outside the restaurant. He'd been in such a good mood starting the evening. Now, somehow, he felt like a chump.

As he drove home, as he flipped channels on television, Reese couldn't get their words out of his mind. He couldn't fire Gabby. She didn't deserve it, and moreover, she had a child and a grandmother depending on her.

He liked her. A lot. But even so, he felt a little damper on his enthusiasm for their getting together the next day.

Could she be enacting some kind of game on him? Or just being kind to a veteran, like those fake people at the restaurant? Had her words around the campfire been a kind lie?

Could a woman really love a man as disfigured as he was?

The next evening, Gabby approached Reese's house and wondered whether she'd made a huge mistake.

For one thing, he lived crazy far out in the woods. She'd been somewhat familiar with the name of his street, which she'd gotten from a quick online search, but she hadn't realized it continued going and going and going, finally turning into a dirt road consisting of two deep, icy ruts.

Her car was *not* happy with her. She only hoped the ancient vehicle wouldn't have half its important parts bounced off.

Of course, getting stuck might be better than arriving, considering what she was here to do. She had to talk to Reese, and it wasn't going to be easy. She'd never told anyone about the assault, except for the therapist she'd talked to at the Christian halfway house and one of the nurses in the delivery room. They'd been women, and strangers, professionally compassionate.

Reese was a whole other story. He'd grown up with Brock, gotten jealous of him because of how much his aunt and uncle gave him while doling out the bare minimum to the nephew they'd been guilted into raising. Oh, he'd never said as much, but he had to feel that way. She'd felt it for him.

So to explain to him that Brock had assaulted her, and that the result had been Izzy...yeah. That was going to be a tough conversation.

Not only that, but she hadn't called a warning, only sent a text. She'd gotten no response. So she didn't know for sure that he would be expecting her.

But they'd planned to get together, and since he'd been busy last night, tonight was what they'd agreed on. Only he'd left the rehearsal today without a word to her, just a cryptic note on her purse saying that he was needed at home.

Had she misread it? His handwriting was terrible, probably a function of him being right-handed but having to use his left hand to write.

And in what sense was he needed at home? Did he have dependents that she didn't know about? A mad wife in the attic like Mr. Rochester of *Jane Eyre* fame?

Don't get hysterical, she scolded herself as she pulled up to a snug cabin, backlit by the rosy glow of sunset. She double-checked the address. Yes, this was his place.

He was probably expecting her. And if he wasn't, if he wasn't even home...well, no denying that would be a big relief, but she'd just have to schedule another get-together.

She needed to talk to him, needed it badly. She had to get the truth off her chest, come what may.

Had to know whether she and Reese had a chance together.

She knocked on his heavy, rough-hewn door, her

heart pounding. What if he told her to get lost? What if he didn't even answer the door?

But no. The door opened, and there he stood, looking at her.

"I texted," she said. "Hope it was okay for me to come out here."

"Not many people do," he said. Then he stepped back and held the door open for her. "Come on in."

"I brought you..." Her hand froze in the act of giving him a plate of cookies. She looked slowly around the room. "Reese, this is amazing."

"These are what's amazing," he said, lifting the plastic wrap to sniff appreciatively at the gingerbread men. "Can I take your coat?"

He was being cordial, which was good, because Gabby was stunned into silence by the beauty of his cabin. The walls, the floor, the ceiling, everything was warm golden wood, softly lit by dim oil lamps. The furniture was rough-hewn, masculine, and she had a sudden notion. "Did you make your couch and chairs yourself?"

He nodded, ducking his head a little. "Just an experiment. Trying to see what I can do with what I have left." He gestured at his partial arm. Again today, he wasn't wearing a prosthesis.

"Looks like you can still do quite a lot," she said, running a hand over the log armrest. Of necessity, the furniture's design wasn't delicate or refined, but then, it wasn't meant to be; this was rugged, outdoorsman furniture, oversize and very masculine.

Like Reese himself.

Then she heard a soft shuffling sound. A small golden dog limped forward, leg bound up.

"Aw, aren't you precious." She dropped to her knees and held out a hand to the dog, who sniffed and then licked it. She looked up at Reese. "Is she yours?"

"Not officially, but…yeah, she probably will be," Reese said. "That's Goldie. She's why I needed to come home."

"What's wrong with her leg? And why didn't she bark when I came in?"

"She just had a second surgery," he explained, "and I need to keep an eye on her. Can't leave her alone too long, but she's not up for the rowdiness of the Rescue Haven dogs." He knelt then, too, and scratched the dog behind the ears until she rolled onto her back, begging for a belly rub. "She was mistreated. We think she might have been shocked with a training collar every time she barked, because she barely makes a sound."

"Poor thing. Who would do that?"

"People who don't want a dog to act like a dog, I guess." He shrugged. "I'm hoping that, with all the squirrels and birds and chipmunks out here, I'll surprise a bark out of her one of these days."

"She's sweet." And so was Reese, for having a heart for vulnerable things. Gabby stroked the dog's soft fur. "I didn't know you had a pet."

"I have a few of them." He pointed to the wall where two large cages stood side by side. "Broken wings, both of 'em." He rolled his eyes as he walked over to show her. "Local wildlife folks have me on speed dial. They found this African gray half frozen a couple of months ago, and the dove just last week."

She lifted an eyebrow. "Somebody thinks you're good with broken wings, eh?"

"I know. It's not exactly subtle." He shrugged. "I

don't mind. I'm not like you, who has a baby and a grandmother—and a brother, for that matter—home needing me."

The reference to Izzy reminded her of the purpose of her visit, but she let herself ignore the reminder. Getting to know this new side of Reese was too interesting. "How do you know how to take care of them? You've never had birds before, have you?"

He shrugged. "Hannah helps me a little, and I do online research." He laughed, sounding self-conscious. "Like I said, I have plenty of time."

Gabby stifled the slight bit of jealousy that flared up at the mention of Hannah's name. Not her business. She needed to pay attention to the casual way Reese referred to her and trust that his more intense responses to Gabby meant something.

Connecting to Reese on a romantic level meant something to *her* now. Meant more and more each day. Meant she was willing to take a pretty big risk to see whether it could happen.

The results, she reminded herself, weren't in her hands. She couldn't control his reaction to her news. Only God could.

The temptation to tell God what to do sure was strong, though.

She looked up from the dove to find Reese studying her. "So…it's nice to see you, but I have the feeling you have a bigger purpose than just bringing me cookies. You must have a reason for wanting to get together."

It flashed through her mind: Couldn't she *just* want to get together with him?

But no, they weren't there yet. And here it went. "I was hoping we could talk," she said. "I thought we just postponed getting together from last night to tonight. Did I misunderstand that?"

"No, that's right," he said. "I just… I just needed to come home and check on these guys." He waved a hand at the animals. But there was something in his voice…

"You sure you weren't avoiding me? Seems like every time we start to get close you back off. Is there something wrong, something I don't know?"

He frowned, paced to the fireplace and stood by the mantel. "I get mixed messages from you."

That was the understatement of the year. "I'm sorry about that," she said. "It's why I wanted to talk to you. But…" She frowned. "I was also sensing some mixed messages from you. I thought you wanted to get together last night, but then you left today as if you didn't."

He looked down at the little dog, picked her up. "My mixed feelings go back a ways," he said. "To the time we were together, and then…we weren't. We've never really talked that through."

"No," she said, "we haven't." She took a deep breath and let it out slowly. "I never really understood what happened."

"I don't want to be harboring old grudges," he said, "but I have to admit, it hurt. I mean, we had what I thought was an agreement, and then…"

Dread clenched Gabby's stomach. Was there something he knew? But how?

"That post," he said. "Brock's post."

She frowned. "What post?"

"Of you and him together. I… Look, there's no denying I was pretty upset."

She stared at him as her stomach started to churn. "I didn't know Brock had posted something about the two of us. I don't even know what he could have posted. When was that?"

"Less than a week after I left," he said quietly.

Before the assault, then. Of course, because Brock's accident had happened immediately after. "If he did, I had nothing to do with it. We certainly weren't dating each other."

"Pictures don't lie," he said. "He had his arm around you and said you were his girl."

A dim memory came back. "I ran into him up at Lake Erie, when we were there with separate groups of friends. I remember him grabbing me and snapping a selfie. I gave him a good scolding for it." Because she hadn't liked him touching her.

Maybe that was another part of what had led to the assault.

"You mean you weren't with him? He said you were his new girl."

"Don't you remember that he tended to say a lot of things that weren't true?" *Like that if I came to that party with him, we could Skype with you.* Gabby grimaced and shook her head. "I honestly couldn't stand him. But you know how he was, always trying to be the center of attention and get people to do what he wanted."

"Oh, yeah. All too well." He blew out a breath. "That makes me feel better, then. I shouldn't have questioned your loyalty that way. I'm sorry."

"So that's why you didn't answer my emails." It was all coming together now. "I thought you were off doing soldier things. At least, until I got your 'leave me alone' message."

He blew out a breath. "I'm sorry. I hope you can forgive me. I should have trusted you over my cousin."

"Reese…" She gathered her courage. "There *is* something I'd like to talk to you about. But it's…hard."

"You don't need to explain anything," he said. He came over to where she was sitting on the edge of the couch and sat down on the ottoman in front of her. "Really. The past is the past, and as long as I know you weren't with Brock—"

As long as I know you weren't with Brock. She swallowed hard, rubbed sweaty hands down her jeans.

Just do it. "I need to say this, for myself if not for you," she said, "if we're to go forward. But I need for you to listen without judging." She coughed and cleared her throat.

He cocked an eyebrow. "I can do that. Want something to drink?"

"Sure." Her throat *was* dry. Even though it would only postpone what was going to be a very hard conversation.

She hadn't known Brock had posted a photo of the two of them together.

Would Reese believe her?

She heard the buzz of her phone, and since Reese was fixing drinks in the small kitchen, she answered it.

"Gabby, Nana's sick," Jacob said. "Can you come home?"

Reese put an arm around Gabby as they watched the EMTs take her grandmother from the ambulance to the ER on a stretcher.

"This is ridiculous," Nana was fuming in a thin, thready voice. "I just need a little extra rest, that's all."

Gabby pressed her hand to her mouth, her eyes filling with tears. "I'm so worried about her! I should never have left her alone."

"You didn't leave her alone," Reese said. "You left her and Jacob together, and Jacob was sensible and called you, and 911, when she fainted."

"She could have broken a bone!"

"Whether you were there or not," he said. "Gabby, this *isn't* your fault."

She nodded slowly. "I suppose you're right. Thanks, Reese."

He knew her well enough to guess what else she was worrying about. "And just now, you were right to leave Izzy with Jacob. She couldn't come to the hospital. And Hannah will be there within a few minutes to take charge. In fact—" he looked down at his flashing phone "—she's already there. She took a pizza. She says Jacob's chowing down and Izzy is fine."

"Thank you." They followed the workers into the ER, and then Gabby got busy with intake paperwork. Reese wasn't a part of the family, so he couldn't go back until Gabby was ready to accompany him, but he was still glad he'd come.

Gabby wasn't one to fall apart, but she'd come pretty close to it when she'd heard her grandmother was ailing. He was just glad he'd been able to help by driving her home, then to follow the ambulance to the regional hospital.

Sheniqua came through the door and he waved her over. She stopped to squeeze Gabby's shoulder and then came over to Reese. "I'm going to check on my patient. You take care of this one—" she nodded sideways toward Gabby "—so she doesn't become a patient herself, okay?"

"Will do." What did it mean that he relished the responsibility?

Moments later they were all in a curtained enclosure in the nearly empty ER. Reese had been hesitant to join them, but they'd all beckoned him in, told him he was like family.

"I'm completely fine," Nana said, and indeed, with the good care she'd received en route, she already sounded much better.

"It looks like you let yourself get dehydrated," Sheniqua said. "That may be all. But while you're here, we're going to run a few tests." She smiled at Nana. "I'll be back in to check on you, okay? You know you're my favorite patient." She patted Gabby's arm on the way out.

"I'm sorry I wasn't there when you got sick." Gabby was holding her grandmother's hand. "I moved here to be available to you and I was gone."

"Gabby—" Reese began, then bit off the words. He didn't want her beating herself up, but this was between Gabby and her grandmother. It wasn't about him.

Nana held up a hand. "Honey," she said, "I couldn't be happier that you and Izzy are living with me, but that doesn't mean you have to save me from every possible thing that could go wrong. I'm *old*," she added with a comical twist of her face.

"No, you're not," Gabby said. "You don't seem old."

"And you'd been recovering so well," Reese added.

"I had," Nana agreed, "but I overdid it with those boys yesterday, and it caught up with me today."

Reese frowned. "I wish you'd told us it was too much." Now *he* was feeling guilty. Nana was so much fun, so high-energy, that it was hard to remember she was in her eighties and had been ill. She might not have the stamina of a younger person.

Around them, low voices and the quiet beeps of machines made white noise, but their curtained enclosure felt private.

"Stop fussing, both of you," she said. "This is minor, but even if it weren't, so be it. I'm not going to be around forever—" she held up a hand to halt Gabby's protest "—and I'm okay with that. I've made my peace with the world and with my life, and I'm ready to meet my Maker when the time comes." She smiled at the two of them. "Although, selfishly, I'd sure like to stick around for a while and see if you two stubborn young people ever see what's right before your eyes."

"What do you..." Gabby broke off, her face reddening.

Heat climbed the back of Reese's neck. Were his feelings for Gabby that obvious? Did she share them?

What had she been about to tell him at his house, right before she'd gotten the phone call about Nana?

She'd seemed nervous and worried about his reaction, which was his own fault. He'd acted judgmental toward her when she'd first returned, sulked around, hadn't wanted to hire her, even.

Now, it was hard to imagine life without her.

He had the feeling she was going to tell him about the circumstances of Izzy's conception, and he wasn't sure he wanted to know. The general outline of it was already clear: she'd gone back to college and fallen into a lifestyle she never would have allowed in Bethlehem Springs. Maybe she'd been drinking at a party or made a mistake about what friends to hang out with. It was understandable. Especially after he'd sent her that cold, harsh message telling her to leave him alone. She hadn't owed him anything.

She didn't owe him anything now, but the question was, did she want to get back together, see what they had? Could she care for him even though he had a significant disability?

That sent his mind back to his aunt and uncle and their concept that he wouldn't appeal to any woman now. They'd been cold to say it, but they might very well be right. He wouldn't want Gabby to have to overcome revulsion in order to embrace him.

Although she hadn't seemed put off when they'd kissed before.

Their idea that he needed to fire her wasn't even worth thinking about. He wouldn't do something so dishonorable.

Yet it was hard to acknowledge that, because of his attitude toward their wishes, Rescue Haven might lose valuable support from his aunt and uncle.

He shook his head, trying to rattle some sense into it. With Gabby worried about her grandmother and the show just around the corner, he needed to be thinking clearly to save his program for the boys and dogs. Wondering and worrying about what would happen with Gabby, about how she felt, did no good.

When he was this churned up, the only thing to do was turn to God. He needed to cast his burdens on the Lord, just as the pastor had recommended a couple of Sundays ago.

While Gabby talked quietly with her grandmother,

Reese bowed his head. *Lord, I'm not sure how all of this is going to turn out, but I could sure use for You to take over. Both with the Rescue Haven program, and with Gabby. Your will be done.*

Of course, he had strong opinions about what *he* wanted done, but that didn't always work out so well. He'd try his best to let go and let God.

Chapter Ten

The next afternoon, back at home, Gabby sat on the edge of her grandmother's bed and tried to manage the mix of love and exasperation she felt. "I'm not leaving you here," she said, keeping her voice firm. "You just got home from the hospital a few hours ago!"

"And she has a doctor to help care for her." Sheniqua tapped on the edge of the bedroom door and then came in. "How are you feeling, Miss Estelle?"

"I'm perfectly fine, except these coddling young people are annoying me. One here and one pacing around the living room like he's going to wear a hole in the carpet."

"I heard that," Reese called.

"We're sorry." Gabby studied her grandmother's face. She did, indeed, look as well as ever. According to the doctors at the hospital, she'd simply overdone it and neglected drinking fluids on the day she'd helped with the boys, and it had caused her to get lightheaded and pass out. All of her tests had come back normal, so she'd been released early that morning with an admonition to pace herself better and stay hydrated.

It was a big relief, but the last thing Gabby wanted to do was to leave Nana alone, or even with Sheniqua.

"You don't have a choice," Nana said firmly.

"That's right," Sheniqua added. "Me and Miss Estelle are going to watch the National Gospel Choir's Christmas concert, and she's going to help me with my knitting project."

"And it might be that I'm working on a project, myself, that you have no business seeing before Christmas. So go on, give a woman some privacy to make a gift for you!"

"But it's your day off!" Gabby said to Sheniqua. "Are you sure…"

"There's nowhere I'd rather spend it." She looked fondly at Nana. "I told you she's my favorite patient. I wasn't kidding."

Gabby looked at Reese, who'd come to stand in the doorway, and shrugged. "I guess we have no choice." And it was a good thing, she supposed. They'd never had the opportunity to resume their conversation. Maybe today was the day.

The idea of talking to him about how his cousin had assaulted her had her quaking with nerves. Reese had been so lovely, helping with Nana. She didn't want to lose the feeling of being even closer to him.

But if that closeness was to be real and ongoing, they couldn't have secrets. So she'd gather her courage and talk to him this afternoon.

Jacob burst into the room, still in his snowy jacket. He'd been throwing sticks for Biff in the snow, and his cheeks were as rosy as apples. "Can you take me Christmas shopping?" he asked Gabby. "Nana was going to, but she can't."

"And pick me up a couple of last-minute gifts," Nana said. "Hand me that pad and pencil and I'll make a list."

"Um, sure." So much for having the time and opportunity to talk to Reese.

"And if you're doing all that," Sheniqua said, "you'd better leave sweet Izzy with us."

"Oh, I couldn't." Gabby stopped in the act of getting the struggling baby into her fleece jacket.

Nana handed her the scribbled list. "Go on, now, and leave the baby to us. We have work to do and a show to watch."

When Gabby hesitated, Nana took her hand. "Let me feel a little useful. Please?"

That was different. "You've got a deal," she said, and handed the baby to Nana.

As they rode into town in Reese's truck, Gabby felt tense but excited. She was worried about Nana and worried about the show…which had been her idea, and if it failed, how would she live with herself?

Most of all, she was worried about telling Reese her secret.

But having that conversation was going to be a lot harder, probably impossible, with Jacob in tow.

Reese pulled in to the last diagonal parking space on Main Street. It was unseasonably warm, and the sun was bright. Icicles dripped from the edges of the buildings and the sidewalks were almost dry of snow, although heaps of it remained along the street.

Dozens of shoppers strolled, looking into shop windows, bundles in hand. The warm weather and clear sky made it a perfect day for last-minute shopping.

The perfect day for a romantic walk with someone

you cared about, too. Gabby's coat sleeve kept brushing against Reese's, making her catch her breath.

She was so aware of him: his easy, athletic stride, the way he waved to people he knew—friendly, but not as if he wanted to stop and talk. He made her feel like he wanted to focus on her, and the sensation was heady.

She even had a little bit of the hero worship she'd felt when they were teenagers together. She was walking downtown with one of the most popular, best-liked football players in town. It upped her status immensely.

And Reese had no clue of how much people admired him, wanted to be his friend.

The back of his hand brushed hers, and the temptation to turn her hand over and interlace her fingers with his was strong, but she didn't do it. Too public of a place…a decision that was validated a minute later when a couple of the Rescue Haven kids came up and started high-fiving Jacob.

In just a short while, he'd become part of the community. He stood up straighter, smiled more readily, sounded more relaxed as he greeted people—other kids and adults alike.

As the other boys walked away, she noticed he was standing straighter still, forking a hand through his hair, the color rising in his cheeks. She turned in the direction he was looking.

Paige.

The pretty teenager stood in front of the window of the pet store, dressed in her stylish jeans and boots, apparently alone.

Gabby's heart clenched up as she watched Jacob suck in a big breath and then head over to her. Her brother wasn't just a kid; he was well on his way to falling in love.

"Hey, Paige," she heard him say in an elaborately casual voice.

"Oh, hey!" Something about the way she said it made Gabby suspect that she'd placed herself in Jacob's path on purpose.

"This isn't good," Reese said quietly to Gabby, and strode over to the teenagers. "Hey, honey. Do your folks know where you are?"

"They know I'm shopping in town," she said, and then turned to Jacob. "Want to hang out?"

He glanced over at Gabby and Reese. "Um, sure, if it's okay with you guys."

Gabby looked at Reese and shrugged. "It's okay with me, if they stay close by."

Reese looked troubled for a moment and then shook his head as if to clear it. "For a little while."

As the teens walked fifty feet in front of them, talking intently, Gabby smiled over at Reese. "Puppy love?"

"Looks like." He glanced over at her. "Brings up some memories, doesn't it?"

Gabby's face warmed. "Yeah. It does."

He didn't say any more, but his steps slowed a little, and she glanced over at him. "What?"

"I really feel like we need to sit down and talk," he said. "I guess now isn't the time, with Jacob, and your grandma, and the show. But right after that, let's you and I make sure we get some private time."

"I'd...like that," she said. And then, because she couldn't stop herself, she asked, "Is anything wrong?"

"Wrong, right, I don't know," he said. "My aunt

and uncle said a few things that I don't think are quite right. Wanted to run them by you."

Dread clenched Gabby's throat, rendering her unable to speak. What had Reese's aunt and uncle been saying to him? What did they know about her?

What did they suspect?

She bit her lip. "I… I do want to talk. We need to. But…" She looked up at him.

"But what?" When she hesitated, he gave her upper arm a little shake. "Don't hesitate or try to protect me. You can say it!"

"Be careful what you ask for," she said. Her voice was shaky and the joking tone she was trying for didn't come through.

Suddenly, a hand clamped down on her shoulder and another on Reese's, and they turned to see Reese's uncle frowning and looking ahead at Jacob and Paige. "What on earth is going on?" he asked.

Reese's heart sank. His aunt and uncle were the last people he wanted to see. He'd been enjoying Gabby's company and feeling close to her. Watching Paige and Jacob's feelings for each other start to grow, he'd been thrown back headlong into the weeks and months when he'd been falling for Gabby, and the memories had been sweet.

Now, though, the feelings he had were based on more. She was a coworker and a mother and a caring sister and granddaughter. In addition to being attracted to her and liking her personality, he now felt admiration for who she was.

But seeing his aunt and uncle brought back all the negative things they'd said when he'd met them for dinner.

He didn't believe that Gabby was a bad person, not in the least. Any bad influencing that had been done in the past had probably gone from Brock to Gabby, not the reverse. Maybe they'd gotten into a little trouble at a party or something, but he couldn't imagine that Gabby had been the wild woman pulling Brock off his pedestal.

The idea that she might be using Reese…that didn't hold water, either. She just wasn't the type. She was a good person. And she certainly more than carried her weight at work.

The only thing that nagged at him was the question of whether she'd be put off by his disability. He'd seen no evidence of that at all, but she might have some hesitations or squeamishness beneath the surface. You couldn't talk yourself out of that.

"I've made it clear," Aunt Catherine said now, "that I don't want Paige hanging around that boy."

Gabby's shoulders stiffened and she turned, slowly. "His name is Jacob," she said.

"Oh, I know his name, and his game. Yours, too."

"What does that even mean?" Gabby sounded bewildered.

"How's your baby?" his aunt asked.

"She's fine. Jacob," she called.

The boy turned, did a double take and said something to Paige. They talked for a minute and then came back toward the adults, reluctance obvious in every dragging step.

"Come on," Gabby said to Jacob. "We need to pick up some things in here." She took his shoulder and steered him into the bookstore, giving a "nice to see you" half wave over her shoulder.

"I need a book, too," Paige said, lifting her chin as if defying her parents to yell at her.

"Not without me, you don't."

"Then you'd better hurry, because I'm going in." And Paige strode into the bookstore, chin held high.

It called to mind Brock, who'd been quick to defy his parents' orders and never suffered a consequence for it.

Reese tapped his aunt's shoulder. "I won't have you being rude to Gabby," he said.

Her eyes widened. "You're telling me what to do?"

"It seems necessary," he said. "Please don't criticize Jacob, either. He's a good kid and he's done nothing wrong."

Aunt Catherine sniffed. "The very idea!" She spun and followed Paige into the store.

The moment the others were out of earshot, Uncle Clive started in. "I see you're still spending time with Gabby. Our offer to help with the Rescue Haven program still stands, but my patience won't last forever."

"I'm losing some patience myself." He smiled briefly at his uncle, more of a grimace, really. "I'm not interested in money that's given to me with those types of strings attached."

"Just wait," Uncle Clive said. "You'll soon see what type of woman Gabby is, and then you'll come crawling back to us, wishing you'd listened."

"Doubtful," Reese said.

Nonetheless, there *were* doubts in his mind. And fears, too. What if the show didn't go well tomorrow and Mr. Romano didn't come through? Would Reese have to take the donation of his aunt and uncle, under their conditions? Would he be able to do that, for the sake of the kids, at Gabby's expense?

Chapter Eleven

Tuesday started off with a bang—literally.

Gabby had just turned her back on Izzy for the time it took to stir the oatmeal. But it was long enough for her to somehow grab on to her old wooden high chair—thankfully she'd been standing beside it, not sitting in it—and knock it over.

Her wails seemed out of proportion, considering that she fell onto her diaper-padded behind at least twenty times per day. Gabby soon saw the reason why. Biff raced through the kitchen holding Izzy's teddy bear high in the air.

"Ba! Ba!" Izzy yelled, her face turning almost purple.

Gabby tried to grab the bear, but she was no match for Biff. "Jacob, could you try to…" She gestured toward the dog, who was now dancing closer, clearly trying to entice Gabby into a game of keep-away.

"I'll get it!" Jacob ran for Biff, who ran away rapidly, head high, tail wagging. The dog moved just fast enough to keep ahead of the laughing Jacob.

"Mercy, what's going on here?" Nana came into the kitchen in her bathrobe, moving slowly.

"Careful, Jacob!" she yelled, but she couldn't get the same message across to Biff, who came perilously close to knocking Nana down.

From the stove came a scorched smell. At the same moment, Jacob yelled, "Something stinks!"

"It's the oatmeal," she said, and hurried over to turn off the gas burner.

"Um, I think it's Izzy." Jacob picked up the baby, inhaled, then wrinkled his nose. "She needs a change."

Patience, Gabby told herself. It had been the subject of the devotional she'd read this morning. Who would have known she'd need to put it into action so quickly?

Once she'd gotten Izzy cleaned, and Nana and Jacob fed with a new batch of oatmeal, she tucked Izzy and Nana in together on the couch with a stack of board books and a pile of warm blankets. Then she hurried Jacob to the barn. Reese had been adamant that he wanted everyone to be on time for their last day of rehearsals before tonight's performance.

She'd disagreed with his having everyone come early—knowing what she knew about Jacob, she'd think teen boys would do better with extra sleep—but he'd been so uptight that she hadn't wanted to argue with him.

When she saw the chaos in the barn, though, she wished she'd spoken up. The younger boys were running around wildly, winding up the dogs and getting them barking. The older boys were spread out in the corners of the barn, sleeping or tapping on their phones.

Paige and her mother walked into the chaos and simply stared.

Jacob looked up, and the blank longing on his face made her heart hurt.

"Hey!" Paige yelled. "Listen up!"

The glamour of Paige had worn off, though, and no one listened.

"Where is Reese?" asked Mrs. Markowski.

Gabby was wondering the same thing. When she walked over and looked at the dogs, she got her answer. He was kneeling in front of Bundi's crate beside Wolf.

"Is she all right?" Wolf asked, his mouth twisted with concern. "Why isn't she coming out?"

"Too many people running around, too much noise. She's confused."

"Hey, everyone, shut up!" Wolf roared, and finally, the boys listened.

"I don't appreciate the way the boys are acting," Paige said to Jacob, her voice snippy.

"It's not my fault," Jacob protested.

"You could at least try to get everyone to calm down."

She sounded almost exactly like her mother. Yikes.

Gabby didn't want to listen in, and Biff gave her an excuse not to by throwing up.

"Oh, he ate a bunch of that burnt oatmeal," Jacob said.

Patience, Gabby reminded herself as she went to get paper towels to clean up after the big dog.

"I have to do some errands," Reese's aunt said stiffly to Gabby as she knelt scrubbing at the floor. "I expect you to keep those two behaving." She nodded toward Jacob and Paige.

"I'll do my best," Gabby promised.

The rest of the morning's rehearsal didn't go much better. When Paige's mother came back to pick her up for a hair appointment she claimed was absolutely necessary, she caught Paige and Jacob kissing in one of the empty stalls. It took all the persuasion Gabby and Reese could muster to keep Aunt Catherine from pulling Paige out of the show.

As the boys went home for dinner and changing, with admonitions to meet at the church at six o'clock sharp, Gabby could see Reese's mouth pulled down in a frown. "It'll be okay," she said.

"How can you be so sure?" he snapped.

"Whoa." She held up her hands. "I'm not sure, not one hundred percent. But dress rehearsals are notoriously bad. They're likely to pull it together for the show."

"I hope so. The whole program is riding on this."

What he didn't say, though he could have, was that that fact was all due to Gabby, who'd come up with the bright idea of putting on a show in a week.

If it failed, it would be on her, and it would affect a lot of boys.

Reese had never been a nail-biter, but he was considering taking it up.

The show was to start in half an hour, and the church's fellowship hall was filling up with people. Most of them were members of the congregation who were here to be supportive and enjoy a little Christmas cheer. But a few were here because of the controversy, the questions Mr. Romano had raised.

"There are a lot of people," Gabby said as she came to stand beside him. "That's good, right?"

"That's good. If it goes well." He didn't want to be too positive, because he'd been at the rehearsals today and he'd seen how ragged the show was.

Mr. Romano had a front-row seat and was sitting with his arms crossed over his chest, not talking to anyone. In fact, no one had taken the chairs on either side of him, probably because he looked so antagonistic.

Great. He was a moody man anyway, and he was clearly in a mood tonight.

All of a sudden, Gabby's grandmother came in and sat down beside Mr. Romano on one side. Bernadette Williams sat down on the other.

Gabby hurried over, and Reese could hear her scolding her grandmother for coming out so soon after being in the hospital.

"That's right, Estelle," Mr. Romano said. "You need to go home. Now."

"I'm just sitting here," she protested. "With my... friends. Isn't that right, Santiago? Aren't we friends?"

An eruption of barking from the backstage area pulled Reese's attention away from Gabby and the others. He strode back to see what was going on.

Biff, who'd been a handful all day, stood barking at the small white dogs who were to serve as lambs. Jacob was yelling at him, exactly what the trainer had said not to do.

Bundi cowered in the back of her crate.

"Jacob," Reese snapped. "You know strategies to handle him. Think, don't just react." Then he rolled his eyes at himself, because he'd reacted rather than thought, yelling at Jacob.

"Oh! Sorry." Jacob tugged Biff away from the white dogs, and when he balked, Jacob snapped his harness on him for better control.

As he tried to switch the leash from Biff's collar to his harness, though, Biff jerked forward, and Jacob lost his grip.

Biff loped out into the crowd, drool hanging from the sides of his huge, panting mouth. Jacob ran after him.

Reese thought of the three elders sitting front and center and rushed after them, until a hand on his arm made him pause.

"Let him handle it," Hannah said.

"But this is dangerous!"

"Biff! Come!" From center stage, Jacob added the special little yodel he'd been using to train Biff, and the dog stopped just a yard short of the horrified-looking Mr. Romano. The big dog spun and ran up the stage stairs to Jacob, dropping into a sit position in front of the boy.

"Yes, good boy!" Jacob handed him a treat as he slid the harness onto him and secured it.

The crowd burst into applause as Jacob led Biff backstage.

Disaster averted, and it was seven o'clock. Show time. Reese trotted up to the stage, welcomed everyone, and explained a little bit about the Rescue Haven program.

Now everyone watched the stage expectantly, but aside from some panicky-sounding voices and the occasional bark from backstage, nothing happened.

Reese's stomach churned. What had they been thinking, letting the boys do a show on so little preparation?

He started to go backstage, but Paige and a couple of the younger boys came out in costume. "While they solve some technical difficulties," Paige said, gesturing behind her, "we wanted to have everyone warm up with a Christmas carol or two. Because we *are* going to ask you to sing during our performance. Does anyone have a favorite?"

Bernadette raised her hand. "How about 'Go, Tell It on the Mountain'?"

"Do we have that?" Paige asked the younger boys.

They pulled out a tablet computer and did some quick scrolling and tapping, and soon the familiar music came through the speakers.

"Will you come up and lead it with me, Miss Bernadette?" Paige asked. "I don't know the words real well."

"I'd be honored." The woman hurried up toward the front and soon had the crowd singing enthusiastically.

When the song was over, Paige and the boys went backstage, and there was again the sound of voices arguing and a dog whining.

Reese's heart rate shot up again. What were they doing back there? No matter how poorly, they had to put on some kind of a show.

He'd have to go back and order them to get started, ready or not. But just as he made that decision, Wolf came out onto the stage and waved his hands for quiet.

"Before we get started, I want to ask for your help," he said. "Can you be real quiet for a minute?"

Lots of nods and curious faces.

He stepped backstage. Seconds later, he emerged holding Bundi in his arms. "This is Bundi," he said, gently rubbing her behind the ears. "She's playing the role of a sheep. A black sheep, I guess."

There were a few chuckles, quickly silenced. "Anyway, she's about fifteen years old from what we know of her background," Wolf said, "and she gets a little confused at times."

"Don't we all," Nana said, and then clapped her hand over her mouth. "Sorry."

"It's okay. She's fine with voices, but loud noises bother her. So when she's out onstage, don't clap and cheer, okay?" He grinned. "If you were planning to clap and cheer. We hope you'll want to." He hesitated, then added, "My great-gram's the same way, forgets some things, but she still likes to be involved, and we love having her involved. Hey, Grammy." He waved to a woman whose wheelchair was parked in the back of the church.

"Say hi, Grammy, it's Wolf." Wolf's mother, standing beside the wheelchair, spoke into the woman's ear, and she gamely lifted a hand in greeting.

Wolf's mom looked teary eyed as she held a hand out to Wolf and then patted her own heart.

The big boy smiled and blew her a kiss. "Anyway, we wanted to let Bundi be involved. She's still a great dog, even though she's old."

There were nods, and smiles and murmurs, and even Mr. Romano uncrossed his arms and looked thoughtful.

Reese realized, with surprise and relief, that the very imperfections of the performance worked to showcase the boys' strengths.

Whether or not they managed to win over their major donor, they'd won Reese over. He was proud of them.

Gabby hovered backstage, straightening costumes and reminding boys of lines until, finally, Jacob ordered her to "go listen, we're fine!"

Then she saw that they needed it to be entirely their

production. She needed to stop interfering. She slipped out to stand beside Reese at the side of the room.

"Everything okay back there?" he whispered as the music started.

"I hope so. They kicked me out."

He reached down and gave her hand a quick squeeze, and she felt it all the way up her arm and into her heart. Working together with Reese on something important, helping boys who had problems, just as they'd both had problems growing up…it meant so much. Maybe too much. That remained to be seen, once she'd had the chance to tell him the whole truth about what had happened after he'd gone to war.

The music built to a loud rap beat, and the shepherds shuffled out, Wolf carrying Bundi, two of the others each walking a white dog.

Several members of the audience looked surprised. It wasn't the music you typically heard in a church, nor the volume.

But Wolf turned to the sound boys and pumped a flat hand up and down, and they lowered the volume.

Good.

They rapped together about the shepherds, seeing a star, getting surprised, agreeing to go. It was ragged; this was the one song Paige wasn't involved with, and it showed.

But the boys were focused and trying. And then Bundi lifted her head and struggled, and Wolf let her down to stand on the stage with the two other dogs. One of the shepherds rolled a ball toward Bundi, slowly, and she caught it in her mouth and then looked surprised. Still rapping, Wolf knelt and petted her, and she dropped the ball into his hand. He rolled it, and she chased after it again. The effect was as if all three dogs were lambs, gamboling together. Perfect, and Gabby could see that the crowd was touched, not least because of the great big boy being so tender with the little dog.

As the shepherds shuffled offstage, leading the dogs, Paige came out. She wore a pale blue head covering and a simple long white dress. She smiled and lifted her arms, and the music of "Angels We Have Heard on High" started to play. "Join in, everyone," she encouraged, and the audience did.

The next scene was in the stable, and the song, while it still had a rap beat, was a bit more melodic thanks to Paige's being the main singer. Gabby glanced around and found the audience rapt. "They're liking it," she said, and squeezed Reese's hand.

This time, they kept their hands clenched together. Which made Gabby's breath go faster. Reese's nearness, the smell of his aftershave, the feel of his callused hand...it was all intoxicating.

At the end of the song, little David stepped forward. "Mary and Joseph were basically homeless," he said, "which means their child was homeless, too." He paused and looked out at his mother, who smiled and nodded encouragingly. "I just wanted to say, my...my family, we've been homeless before, too, and it's hard."

Gabby could hear several people around her murmuring in apparent surprise.

David knelt and picked up one of the white dogs. "This is Blanca, and she's been homeless, too. They found her running around on the street, and you couldn't even tell she was a white dog at first."

As if she knew she was the center of attention,

Blanca sat perfectly straight. Then, at a gesture from David, she rose onto her back legs into a begging position, and he rewarded her with a treat.

Gabby squeezed Reese's hand, blinking back tears.

"Sometimes when you're homeless, you feel worthless," David went on. "But to think that Jesus, the savior of the world, spent some time that way...well, it makes you feel better."

Blanca let out one sharp bark as if to agree.

David left the stage, leading Blanca, and the audience burst into applause.

Paige led them in "Away in a Manger," and Gabby saw several people wiping tears.

The final song was a rap about Jesus as Lord, and yet a kid.

"You wouldn't think a kid could make a difference, but he did," was the chorus.

And as Gabby looked around, she saw that these children *were* making a difference. "They're making a difference because of you," she whispered to Reese.

"And you," he whispered back.

In his eyes, she saw mirrored the same happiness and joy she felt herself. And as the whole room swept into a moving version of "Silent Night, Holy Night," and the boys all came out to sing and then take their bows, she was deeply moved.

She was so, so glad she'd come home. So glad she'd been persuaded to work with Reese.

So excited about whatever might come next.

Chapter Twelve

Reese breathed a sigh of relief as the applause died down and people started heading to the back of the room, where the cookies, hot chocolate and excited boys were.

Judging from Mr. Romano's reluctantly impressed face, they'd pulled it off. After that initial series of glitches, the presentation had gone well. The boys were endearing and talented, and Paige had brought both beauty and dignity to her role. The dogs had behaved as well as could be expected, and even Biff, firmly restrained by Jacob, had earned applause by raising a paw to the congregation to wave goodbye.

Gabby was talking to Bernadette Williams and another board member Reese didn't know. It looked like a lovefest, and Gabby was smiling ear to ear, obviously enjoying herself. So when one of the teenage helpers came in from the nursery with Izzy, Reese offered to take charge of her. He walked through the gathering with the baby against his chest, greeting people, accepting their congratulations and questions, but always aware of Gabby.

The weight of little Izzy, the clean, baby-shampoo smell of her, the way she laughed and pulled at his ear, all of it tugged at his heart. He'd never been one of those guys who was a natural with babies, but Izzy was special. Extra sweet, just like her mama. He dropped a kiss on the top of her head.

He couldn't wait to share with Gabby his thoughts and opinions about how the show had gone, to laugh with her and hear what people had said.

All of a sudden Marla Evans, one of his aunt's friends, stepped directly in front of him, blocking his path. "I admire you, Reese," she said.

The compliment was surprising enough that he didn't back away immediately as he might otherwise have. He'd seen Marla stir up trouble too often to be one of her fans, and he'd certainly never heard her say anything positive about him. But maybe the show had affected her. "What would cause you to admire me, Marla? It's the boys who deserve your admiration, not me."

"That's not what I'm talking about." She pursed her artificially enhanced lips. "I don't know if I should say what I *am* talking about."

"Up to you." Reese guessed he had to be nice to the woman. After all, they were in church. He inhaled the scent of pine and candles and sugar cookies, listened to the sound of people talking happily. Everyone was excited about the holiday, and it was good to see.

"You're so forgiving," Marla said.

He frowned. "Am I?" He looked over her head, scanning for Gabby, not wanting her out of his sight.

"To be so friendly with the girl who was with your cousin the night he died."

"Say *what*?" He was only half listening.

"Oh, I don't blame her for it the way a lot of people do, but if she hadn't fought with poor dear Brock... who knows? He might be here with us now."

"Wait a minute." Reese focused on what Marla was saying. "Gabby was with Brock on the night he..."

"Oh, you didn't know?" The delight of a natural gossip crossed her face. "Yes, apparently they had quite an argument. Lovers' quarrel, I guess. Such a shame."

Brock and Gabby hadn't had a lovers' quarrel. They hadn't been lovers. The very idea of Marla saying that annoyed Reese. Perhaps sensing his tension, Izzy stirred in his arms, arching her back as she looked around. She must want her mother.

And Reese wanted away from this conversation.

Marla held out a hand toward Izzy and patted her head. When Izzy twisted away from the unfamiliar touch, Marla ran a finger over the baby's face. "Poor little fatherless thing. She looks so much like her— like Brock."

Reese had been turning away, but he stopped. "What did you say?"

Marla looked him directly in the eyes. "She looks a lot like Brock."

Time itself seemed to stop, and the room seemed to go silent, and all he could see was Izzy's face.

A face that looked so much like his cousin's that he was amazed at his own stupidity for never having seen it before.

He hadn't realized that Gabby had been with Brock on the night he'd died. It made sense; after all, Brock had posted a photo of himself with Gabby not long before that night.

But the fact that Izzy looked so much like him…

He mumbled out some kind of a "see you later" to Marla. As if he were moving through thick cotton, he made his way over to Gabby, who now stood on the edge of the crowd. People still spoke to him, but he couldn't process their words, couldn't take the time to respond in a socially correct manner.

When he reached Gabby, now standing a little apart from everyone else, she brushed back her hair and smiled up at him, that sweet, intimate smile.

It made him furious.

He thrust Izzy into her arms. "Why did you lie to me?"

"About what?" The smile slid from her face.

"You know what." He gestured toward the baby. "About her." Then, when she still looked confused, he spelled it out. "About her father. He wasn't a college boy at all, was he?"

A part of him hoped she'd get angry, defend herself, ask him what he was talking about. But she didn't, of course. Instead, she looked at the floor, half turned away. "Reese, I…" She broke off.

Heat surged from his cracked-open heart. "What everyone says is right," he spat out. "You're a liar, from a family of liars."

He'd thought he was speaking softly, but the murmurs around him started to come through. If people couldn't hear what they were saying, they could probably detect the tone. He looked around at a blur of faces and homed in on one: Jacob's, closer than the rest, full of raw pain.

That made his heart lurch, but he couldn't be bothered with worry for the boy when his fury at Gabby was so fresh, so sharp.

He looked at Gabby again. Tears were leaking from her eyes. Crocodile tears. But she was saying nothing in her own defense.

"Aren't you even going to answer me?" he demanded.

She brushed the tears from her face and lifted her chin. "You have no idea what you're talking about," she said loud and clear, "and no right to ask me questions."

What an amazing amount of gall she had. "We're through." He wanted to say more, but he didn't trust himself to stop if he got started. Instead, he turned and stormed out of the church.

Gabby's heart felt torn in two as she watched Reese go. There had been fury in every line in his face, and now, his rigid back and fast strides spelled out control on the very edge.

Izzy shifted and arched her back, then broke into a loud cry. If every eye in the church hadn't been on Gabby before, it was now as she tried without success to calm her baby.

She just wanted to curl in on herself and weep. Weep for the loss of what she'd foolishly allowed herself to hope for: that Reese cared about her, the real her. That he would accept her and might with time be able to hear and deal with the truth.

But she couldn't think about her own pain, because Izzy was wailing inconsolably now, no doubt picking up on the tension in the room. She propped her daughter on her shoulder and headed toward the ladies' room, head down, avoiding people's eyes. Maybe she just needed a diaper change. And maybe time away from all these people would calm Gabby down, too.

As she reached the edge of the room, someone tapped on her shoulder.

It was Hannah, studying her with concern on her face. "Hey, you okay?"

Gabby nodded, not trusting her voice.

Hannah fell into step beside her, and Gabby didn't know how to tell her she wanted to be alone.

"Listen, this is none of my business," Hannah said, "but Marla Evans was talking to Reese a few minutes ago, and the two of them had words."

So that was how Reese had found out. From a town gossip.

"Whatever they were arguing about," Hannah continued, "it didn't just upset Reese, it upset your brother, Jacob. He came over to talk to you, but then Reese got there first. Jacob heard everything you were talking about, and it looked like he got even more upset. You might want to talk to him."

"Okay. Thanks for telling me." They were in the ladies' room now, and Gabby put Izzy down onto the changing table and did a quick diaper change without looking at Hannah.

Why didn't the woman leave so Gabby could cry?

Hannah cleared her throat. "I mean, really upset him. You might want to find him sooner rather than later. Do you want me to hold the baby?"

She looked so doubtful that Gabby almost smiled. "It's okay, I can take her with, but thanks." She wondered what Reese and Marla had been talking about.

Was Jacob upset because they'd been trashing Gabby or talking in a mean way about Izzy's parentage?

She thanked Hannah again as she left the bathroom, then started searching the church halls. Just as well that she had something to do, someone to take care of, so she didn't have to go over and over the things Reese had said to her.

The church was quieting down now; most people had gone home. Back in the fellowship hall where the show and reception had taken place, she could hear murmuring voices, the sound of dishes clinking and chairs being stacked. People were cleaning up.

She turned a corner and there was Jacob by the coatrack, shrugging into his coat. His lips were pressed in a tight line and the freckles stood out on his pale face. "Hey," she said. "You okay?"

She expected him to deny his feelings like most fifteen-year-old boys would. Instead, he faced her, eyes blazing. "Reese said our family is a bunch of liars."

Her heart lurched and she reached out to touch Jacob's arm. "I know it hurts to be accused like that, but he wasn't talking about you. He was talking about me."

Jacob shook his head. "Don't cover it over. We're losers. You, me and Mom, at least."

"Jacob—"

But he shook off her arm and spun away.

"You can walk home, but nowhere else," she called after him as he ran out of the church.

Gabby pulled Izzy close and sank down onto a chair beside the door. She'd handled all of this terribly, and now Jacob, too, was being hurt by it. In trying to protect Reese and his family from the truth about Brock, she'd hurt others who didn't deserve it.

She needed to find Reese and talk with him, but her heart sank at the impossibility of making him understand. She shouldn't give in to the shame that kept wanting to wash over her. In her head, she knew the fault lay with Brock and not with her, that her mistake of trusting him didn't mean she deserved what had happened. But her strength and belief in herself were so shaky. A scornful look and angry words from Reese had swept them away.

Reese. His fury felt worse than anyone else's ever could, because she'd felt so close to him. She'd started to let him into her heart.

A mistake she couldn't make again.

Izzy against her shoulder, she bowed her head and prayed for discernment and wisdom and the right action to take next.

Chapter Thirteen

Reese was in his car, driving too fast and without a destination. He wanted to get away from the idea of Gabby being with his cousin, but the images in his mind were inescapable.

He'd seen them together with his own eyes, or at least, a picture of them on social media, and Gabby had admitted it was accurate, though she'd explained it away. She'd lied, though, saying she didn't even like Brock, had never liked him, found him mean.

Not too mean to give yourself to and conceive a child with. If Brock hadn't had an accident, would he and Gabby be married by now? What had they been arguing about at that party on the night of Brock's accident? Had Gabby broken the news that she was expecting?

If she'd been carrying *Reese's* child, nothing would have given him greater joy. No matter what the circumstances.

But that wasn't going to happen. Even though, on some level, he'd been fool enough to think about raising a child with her. Something about being around her and the boys, seeing how well she handled them, had planted that seed in his head.

He shook his head but the thoughts wouldn't quiet. He pushed harder on the accelerator and the tires spun on the icy road.

He forced himself to slow down. He had to be responsible, to stay safe. The boys needed him, even if Gabby didn't.

His phone buzzed on the seat beside him and he ignored it, but as soon as the call cut off it started buzzing again.

Was it Gabby?

He hated himself for hoping it was.

The car skidded a little again. Clearly he couldn't drive away from his troubles. He found a safe place to turn around, the empty parking lot of a little machine shop, and grabbed his phone.

Was it Gabby?

She wouldn't dare. If she called him, he'd block her number.

But it wasn't Gabby's number, and the disappointment that slumped his shoulders made him angry. It was his cousin, Paige, and she could wait.

But the call came again, and he sighed and clicked into the call. "Hey, Paige, what's up?"

"You've got to get over here to the house," she said.

"Paige, I can't—"

"It's an emergency. Mom and Dad are going off the rails." She said something to someone, and there was shouting in the background. "Hurry," she said, and ended the call.

His aunt and uncle going off the rails about this or that was nothing new. But it wasn't as if he had anything else to do. For better or worse, his aunt and uncle and Paige were his family, and he'd moved back here in part to be there for them. He put the car into gear, tamped down all the hurt and anger inside him and drove back toward town.

Gabby clicked out of her phone call and quickly recounted to Nana what Paige had told her.

"Go, go, I'll take care of the baby." Nana took Izzy in her arms and waved Gabby toward the door. "Go help your brother." She sat down heavily in her old recliner and rocked, clicking her tongue at Izzy, whose cries grew quieter.

"I don't like leaving you alone here when you're so tired." And sick. And old looking. Nana's face seemed to sag, and she let out a racking cough, turning her face away from Izzy.

The news that Jacob was in trouble had hit her harder than she was letting on, and Gabby was torn. Which one needed her help more?

She sent a quick text to Hannah, who instantly agreed to come over and sit with Nana until Gabby could get back.

"You'd better go." Nana's eyes watered a little, which shocked Gabby, because she'd seen Nana cry only once or twice. "I'd go myself, but I can't drive at night. I need for you to take care of this."

"I will." Even though the Markowskis' mansion was the last place on earth she wanted to be.

Oh, Jacob, what have you done?

When she pulled up in front of the house, the harassed-looking police officer looked relieved. "Are you his legal guardian?"

"I'm his sister." She walked over to Jacob, in hand-cuffs beside the officer, and put her arm around his shoulder. "What did he do that you have to restrain him like this? He's a juvenile."

"He tried to run away from us, ma'am." The officer turned to the Markowskis, who were standing shoulder to shoulder on the front walk of their home, faces drawn tight. "Since it's cold out and the perpetrator is a juvenile and restrained, we might be more comfortable if I take everyone's statements inside."

The last thing Gabby wanted was to walk into the Markowski home, where she hadn't been since a couple of short visits when she was a teenager. She still thought of it as Brock's home.

But Jacob was shivering, and so was Mrs. Markowski, despite her fur-collared coat.

"Come in, Mom, Dad! It's freezing out here!" Only then did Gabby realize that Paige was standing on the porch behind her parents, arms wrapped around herself, shivering.

Mr. Markowski put a hand on each of his wife's shoulders and turned her around. "Come on, Catherine. We'll sit in the living room and give our statements. And you—" he pointed at Paige "—you don't need to be here. You go to your room."

"He needs an advocate!" Paige protested. "He didn't really do anything and you're making it sound like he's a criminal!"

Relief washed over Gabby. If Paige didn't think whatever Jacob had done was serious, it probably wasn't.

"I'd rather not have either of those two in my home."

Mrs. Markowski waved a dismissive hand at Jacob and Gabby, as if they were dirt.

Gabby squeezed Jacob's shoulder tighter and they followed the police officer inside.

They bypassed the elegant living room and trooped into the den, where Gabby sat down beside Jacob on the sofa when directed to do so by Mrs. Markowski. Mr. and Mrs. Markowski sat in a pair of leather chairs, and the police officer took out his tablet and sat on the ottoman. The Markowskis gave their indignant statements—they'd come home from church to discover their expensive lawn decorations knocked over and Jacob in the process of ripping down the lights from their bushes, lights that had taken their gardener *hours* to put up.

Gabby stayed close to Jacob. "When it's your turn, tell the truth," she said quietly.

"She's coaching him!" Mrs. Markowski objected.

The police officer ran a hand over his face. "Let's just get the basic facts down for now," he said. "Young man, let me hear what happened from you. And your sister's right—tell the truth."

Jacob tonelessly described what he'd done, refusing to give a reason for it, and Gabby looked around the room to avoid the Markowskis' mean, accusatory eyes.

When she saw the built-in bookshelf, her heart rate increased along with her breathing.

It was everything Brock. His football jersey, framed. A shelf full of trophies. Worst of all, his senior picture, enlarged and lit with a small lamp beneath the frame.

He seemed to be sneering down at her. She could almost hear his voice: "You're worthless. No one will believe you. You're trash like your mother, your whole family."

All the things he'd said before and during the assault seemed to ring in her ears, things she'd pushed out of her consciousness. A wave of nausea washed through her, and she hunched over, arms wrapped around herself.

Here she was in Brock's fancy living room, listening to her brother admit to committing a crime.

Breathe. You can live through this, she reminded herself. *You've lived through something much harder. Breathe.*

It can't get any worse.

She drew in a deep breath, let it out slowly, drew in another. The nausea started to recede.

Then the door opened and Reese walked in.

Reese looked at the tableau before him and felt like turning right around and walking back into the night. Why hadn't he kept driving?

Did he really have to deal with Gabby again tonight?

But the ashamed, miserable look in Jacob's eyes, the slump of the boy's shoulders, told him that, yes, he had to stay. Had to stay right here in his cousin's house with the woman who'd chosen his cousin over him, and conceived a child with him.

He had to stay because he remembered being just like Jacob, thought of as a criminal, assumed to be the bad guy.

"What's going on?" he asked wearily, avoiding Gabby's eyes.

His aunt and uncle chimed in with descriptions of

the boy's horrible crime of defacing their expensive Christmas decorations.

The police officer stood. "I think we have all the information," he said, cutting off the rant. "It's up to you whether to press charges."

"Don't press charges," Reese said automatically. "I'm sure Jacob can do something to pay for the damage."

"Yes, of course. We can pay for the damage, and Jacob will work until he's repaid the money," Gabby said. There was only a slight tremor in her voice, and Reese figured he knew why: there went her Christmas funds.

But he didn't need to be feeling sorry for her, not after the betrayer she'd shown herself to be.

"We most certainly are pressing charges," Aunt Catherine said.

Reese looked at his uncle and saw a little more reason there. "Does it have to be decided tonight? Why don't you wait and sleep on it. I can help put the decorations back up."

"Not much going to happen between now and Christmas," the officer contributed. "I can release him to his sister's care, but that makes you, ma'am, responsible for keeping him out of trouble until we can get this sorted out."

"He'll stay out of trouble." She nudged Jacob. "Do you have anything you want to say to the Markowskis?"

Reese wanted to warn her that Jacob was in no mind-set to apologize—again, speaking from experience—but to his surprise, Jacob lifted his chin. "I'm sorry I messed up your decorations. I'll pay you back."

"Good man," Reese said, still not looking at Gabby.

"He'll lie to get what he wants," Uncle Clive said.

"You're free to go, ma'am," the officer said. "We'll be in touch right after the twenty-fifth."

"Thank you." She turned and led Jacob out.

The look she gave Reese as she passed was pure misery. But it didn't move him, no way.

He wasn't surprised his uncle thought Jacob was a liar. The whole family were liars. He stepped back and didn't speak as they walked out the door.

Gabby didn't have the heart to lecture Jacob on the way home. She was too busy trying not to weep.

Being in the Markowski home and seeing the pictures of Brock—a memorial set up to him, as if he'd been some kind of hero—made her almost physically ill. But it also brought home the fact that the whole family wanted and needed to believe the best of their lost son. Understandable, and what harm did it do, when Brock wasn't alive to assault any other women?

They pulled up outside Nana's house, and Gabby turned off the car and sat. Jacob didn't make a move to go in, either.

As the big sister, she ought to have wise words. But what came out was "You okay?"

He turned his head to look at her. "Sure."

The single word was obviously untrue. "Tough being from a family known for bad things, isn't it? Kind of makes you want to live up to the rumors."

"Yeah." He looked sideways at her. "Who's Izzy's father, really?"

Gabby closed her eyes. "I can't say."

"Sure." He shrugged, opened the car door and headed through the biting snowfall toward the house.

Her arms and legs felt too heavy to move, but she forced them to. Nana was inside with Izzy, and she had to be tired. Gabby couldn't ignore her responsibilities.

When she got inside, though, Izzy was asleep in her crib in Gabby's room. Nana was ushering Jacob into his room, talking to him in a low voice, and Hannah had apparently gone home. So Gabby was free to go to bed herself.

She did, and then the tears came.

No way could she work with Reese anymore, so she was out of a job. She didn't want to get Jacob in even more trouble by involving his father, asking him for money. That meant she had to front Jacob the money to pay back the Markowskis, so there went any money she could've spent to make a nice Christmas for Izzy, as well as for Nana and Jacob.

She heard Nana walk slowly down the hall to her bedroom, coughing, the same horrible cough she'd had when Gabby had first arrived. So she was back to where she'd been.

Gabby hadn't done any good at all since she'd arrived. She'd only made things worse. She looked at Izzy sleeping in her crib and, for once, let herself remember dark days before and right after she'd been born. The misery of the pregnancy, all alone, dodging people's questions. Giving birth in a clinic without anyone there to hold her hand, not having a clue as to how she was going to manage.

If it hadn't been for a wonderful Christian halfway house, she could very well have ended up on the streets.

Only when there was a light tap on the door did

Gabby realize that tears were streaming down her cheeks.

"May I come in, dear?" Nana asked.

She grabbed for tissues. "Just a minute." She wiped her eyes and blew her nose and went to the door, but the sight of her grandmother's kind, concerned face made the tears come again. "I'm sorry," she said, not wanting to add more stress to Nana's worries. Jacob's problems were enough to contend with. "Just an emotional day. I'll be fine."

"Of course you will, dear," Nana said. "But sometimes, it helps to talk about what's bothering you. That's what I'm here for."

Gabby felt a great longing to share with Nana what had happened all those years ago. To confide in someone who wasn't a trained counselor but a family member who cared about her. To share the pain and humiliation and be reassured that she was still all right, still loved.

"What is it, honey?" Nana took her hand and sat down beside her on the bed.

"Oh, Nana." She sighed. "You don't want to know."

"I do want to know. What's bothering you so much? Jacob got in a little trouble, but we'll manage it."

"It's not that."

Nana lifted an eyebrow and watched her steadily.

"Do you remember…" she began, then faltered.

"Remember what?"

"Do you remember, after Reese left…I went to a party?"

Nana frowned. "You went to a lot of parties over the years."

"This one was with…with Brock." She swallowed.

"Oh, yes, that I do remember. You were going to do a video call with Reese. Come to think of it, I don't remember if you ever got through or not."

"We didn't." She drew in her breath with a gasping, sobbing sound.

Nana gripped her hand tighter. "Tell me what happened."

She blew out a breath, sucked in another. "Brock took me into one of the bedrooms. So we could have quiet, to talk to Reese. That's what he said."

Nana's eyebrows drew together. "Go on."

"Only we didn't talk to Reese. Instead, he…" She bit her lip and looked off to the side. "He raped me, Nana."

A strangled sound came from Nana's chest, and then she pulled Gabby to her and held her tightly. "Oh, my poor girl. My poor, poor girl."

The sympathetic words and the warm embrace loosened what was left of Gabby's tears.

Nana let her cry, rocking her back and forth. "And that's how Izzy came to be."

Gabby nodded.

"Did anyone know?" she asked when the tears slowed down.

Gabby shook her head. "He said no one would believe me. I fought him, Nana. And though I couldn't keep him from doing what he did, I screamed at him afterward. I was as angry as I was scared. But that was the night—"

"The night he wrecked his car and died." Nana's words sounded heavy. "Oh, my dear. I am so very sorry."

"And Reese," she choked out. "Reese just realized

tonight…someone just told him…that Izzy looks like Brock. So he came and accused me of cheating on him with his cousin. I don't know what to do."

Nana pulled away enough to stare at Gabby. "He's throwing stones without knowing the circumstances." Two high red spots colored her cheeks. "I'd like to give that boy a piece of my mind."

"Don't tell him, Nana," Gabby said, alarmed at her grandmother's obvious high emotions. Nana didn't need any more stress. "It's okay. All's well that ends well. I have Izzy. *We* have Izzy. And if Reese is that narrow-minded and judgmental, well, I guess I don't want him." She made her words firm, almost firm enough to convince herself. Not quite, but almost.

"I want you to rest," Nana said to her. "You've had a hard night and spilled a lot of emotion. You just sleep in here with your baby and don't think one thought about men, all right?"

A smile creased Gabby's face. She was in her twenties and a mother, but being cared for by Nana still felt good.

Nana helped her lie down and pulled the covers up under her chin. "You just rest, dear. Everything is going to be all right."

It wasn't. Her heart wasn't going to be all right, not quite, not ever. But Gabby nodded and let her grandmother think she'd made it all better, just like when Gabby was small.

Reese arrived at the church early for Christmas Eve services, mysteriously directed to do so by Gabby's grandmother.

He just hoped she wasn't trying to set up a ridiculous reconciliation. It was the kind of thing she'd do—like how she'd as much as forced him to hire Gabby. *And look how that had turned out.*

If she brought Gabby in and tried to get them together, he'd be hard-pressed to be polite.

But when he arrived in the little church parlor to find Nana there all alone, his heart sank and he realized: some part of him had hoped to find a way things could be repaired with Gabby.

He was a fool.

Nana didn't smile. "Sit down," she said, gesturing at a chair set up to face her.

He felt like he was at a tribunal, especially with the religious paintings surrounding them, the smell of candles, the dim light.

"I understand you're angry at Gabby." Her words were tight, clipped.

"Well…yes. Yes, I am. But that's between us."

"The two of you are making a botch of it! Now listen." The old woman leaned forward. "Love is too wonderful and rare to waste on a misunderstanding."

She was making him sound petty. *Feel* petty. "Lying and deception are more than a misunderstanding."

"So is being judgmental," she said severely. "I take it your hostility has to do with Izzy's father?"

He didn't want to admit to it, but he couldn't deny those clear, uncompromising eyes.

"You're angry because you think it's your cousin, Brock."

He blew out a breath, leaned forward and propped his cheek on his clenched fists, nodding. "Yeah."

Then he waited for her to deny it. Hoped she would. Hoped Marla's information had been wrong.

"Well. I learned last night that you're right." Nana lifted her chin. "Your cousin Brock was Izzy's biological father."

Rage and despair propelled him out of his chair. "Is that what you wanted to tell me?" He got so far as turning toward the door before his manners turned him around. "Is that all?"

"Sit down," she ordered.

He should have kept walking. He definitely didn't want to listen. But you treated your elders with respect, so he sat back down.

"How well did you know your cousin?"

He shrugged. "Pretty well. We grew up together, from the time I was twelve."

"How would you describe his personality?"

He shrugged again. "Athletic. Well liked."

She actually rolled her eyes at him. "Not on the surface. I mean his inner self."

Reese thought about his cousin, and the words that came out were "Entitled and mean."

Nana nodded. "That was my impression, too."

They sat a moment in silence. Reese looked at his knees, thinking of his cousin. Tragic that he'd died, of course, and it had broken his aunt's heart. But there was no personal sense of loss inside of Reese. He'd stopped trusting his cousin within six months of living with him, if he'd ever even started. He'd kept the peace, played on sports teams with him, listened to his exploits and complaints. But he had to admit he'd never liked Brock. Never trusted him.

Which made it sting all the more that Gabby had chosen to give Brock what she wouldn't give to him.

What they'd agreed to wait for, before sharing with only each other.

He looked up to find Nana watching him. "Does Brock seem like the kind of man Gabby would choose?"

The question stopped his racing thoughts cold. Slowly, he shook his head. "No. He doesn't. That's why it's so crazy that—" He broke off because Nana was pushing herself up out of her chair, and he hurried to help her.

"You're right," she said once she was steady on her feet. "He isn't the type of man Gabby would choose."

Her words circled in his head as she walked toward the parlor door. "Wait, Nana. What did you just tell me?"

"Think it through, Reese. Think of the times when choice is taken away from a woman. Ever heard of that?"

He had, of course, but… "I don't get it."

"She would never have chosen Brock," Nana said patiently. "But what if she didn't have a choice?"

"If she didn't have a…" He trailed off, because the only reason Gabby wouldn't have had a choice about Brock as the parent of her child was if… He looked into those clear eyes. "He didn't…force her…did he?"

She just gave him another steady look and then walked slowly out of the room.

Minutes later he was striding through the church. If he'd been angry before, now he was furious, outraged…*for* Gabby, not at her. He had to find her, to tell her he understood, that he'd been wrong.

There she was, among the crowd of people starting to file into the sanctuary. He approached her, put a hand on her shoulder. "Gabby, wait."

She turned. Izzy was in her arms, and Gabby was wearing a red dress he remembered her wearing in high school. And dignity, wrapped around her like a cloak. "I don't want to talk to you," she said, and walked into the church.

He couldn't stop her, couldn't force her to listen to him. She'd been forced enough and had survived on her own incredible strength.

His mind kept circling around the truth Nana had shown to him, a truth that immediately felt accurate.

Of course Gabby wouldn't choose Brock. She'd never liked him.

And Brock... Gabby wasn't exactly his type, but he'd always felt entitled to take whatever he had a momentary whim for.

Reese didn't live in a hole; he knew how many women had faced harassment or worse. Stories were everywhere in the media, which had to mean there were ten times as many stories that hadn't been publicly told.

He'd never even considered the fact that Gabby's story could be one of them.

How could he let her know he was sorry for misjudging her? How could he make it up to her? What was he going to do?

He couldn't face sitting alone through the church service nor standing out here schmoozing with merry parishioners over hot chocolate and Christmas cookies. He ducked into the church's tiny, empty chapel and let the door close behind him.

He sank down into a back pew and let his head drop

into his hands. At his wits' end, full of shame for the wrong he'd done Gabby, and anger at the wrong that had been done to her, he lifted an inarticulate prayer to God.

He didn't expect any answers. He'd acted like scum, didn't deserve direction from God. After long, contrite moments, he opened his eyes, leaned back and looked around the little chapel.

What caught his eye immediately was a banner.

To know the love of Christ, which passes knowledge, that you might be filled with all the fullness of God. Ephesians 3:19.

He knew that. Knew he was loved, because God loved everyone.

Except…it had always seemed like God loved some people better than others. He'd always thought Brock was better, more loved, because that was how it had been in his aunt's home.

But his conversation with Nana had made him think.

Brock *wasn't* better. Of course not. He was a blustering, mean-spirited bully who had done the worst thing possible to Gabby. Even now, Reese's blood boiled at the thought of it, and he pounded his fist on the back of the pew.

There was nothing he could do to exact revenge, but he sure wanted to.

Sitting a little longer in the chapel, though, he remembered that vengeance belonged to the Lord.

Of course. Brock had gone to meet his maker immediately after the horrible thing he'd done. Reese had made plenty of mistakes in his own life, had sometimes dreaded having to defend his life before God, but he'd done nothing on the scale of what Brock had done. He had to figure that God knew how to take care of that.

Probably the worst thing Reese had done, now, was to mistrust Gabby and say mean things to her. He prayed about that, asked for forgiveness.

Knew he could be forgiven by God, already was.

Gabby, though…that was another question. She saw into people's hearts.

So making sure his heart was right—that was the important thing.

He sat staring at that banner, read it again.

To know the love of Christ, which passes knowledge, that you might be filled with all the fullness of God. Ephesians 3:19.

He *knew* the love of God, in his head at least, but did he really *know* it in his heart? Was he filled with the fullness of God?

He had to admit the truth: not really. Some of the time, maybe, but not all the time. Not enough to make him good at dealing with life's challenges and blows.

He had the feeling, though, that Gabby truly knew that love. Otherwise, how could she deal with what had happened to her? His stomach twisted at the very notion.

How could she raise Brock's child, but by an exceptional gift of grace from God?

He sat praying for some of that kind of love and grace to fill him, too, until the heightened music let him know the service had ended. Then he went to Gabby's car to wait for her.

When Gabby emerged from the church into snow-flakes that looked as big as saucers, Izzy lifted her face, felt them and blinked, looking startled. Then she laughed and tried to catch them.

Gabby stepped back to take Nana's arm, intending to give her a little extra support on the slippery sidewalk, but Nana was talking to Mr. Romano. They were arguing, of course, but amicably for once.

After Mr. Romano's family came and swarmed around him, Gabby took Nana's arm and walked with her to the car.

At which point she saw Reese leaning against it, arms crossed, legs planted wide. He looked like a movie star to her, and her heart turned over.

He might be handsome, but it was how a man treated you that mattered. She stopped, clutching Izzy a little tighter. "What do you want?"

"I'm still hoping to talk to you," he said.

Nana looked over at Gabby, her grip tightening. "I can take Izzy home, if Reese can bring you. If you want to talk to him, that is."

She frowned and shook her head. "I don't think so."

Reese took a step toward her. "Gabby, I'm so sorry for not delving into the real story of what happened…" He broke off, took a breath. "What happened with Brock."

Gabby narrowed her eyes at Nana. "You told him!"

"I just put a few facts into his mind. He figured out most of it himself," Nana said complacently.

She studied Reese. His eyes were sympathetic, sure. But something still didn't feel right about all of this. Gabby needed to listen to her own truth, not anyone else's. "Reese," she said, "I'll think about forgiving you. I appreciate your apology. But honestly, I've heard sweet words from you before, and they were quick to change once something else happened that made you think badly of me." She shook her head slowly. "Words are cheap. They're not enough." She sidled past him to open the car door, snapped Izzy into her car seat and then helped Nana into the passenger seat.

She got into the driver's seat. Carefully, she eased the car out of its parking space and drove away from the man she loved with all her heart.

Chapter Fourteen

As Reese drove to his aunt and uncle's house, he berated himself. Why hadn't he ever considered that Gabby might have gotten pregnant through an assault? When he thought it through, he realized anew how committed she'd been to saving intimacy for marriage. She'd been tempted during their high school relationship, they both had, but she'd stood strong against it and encouraged him to do the same. They'd avoided situations where too much willpower would be required. They'd talked about it and prayed about it.

So why hadn't he instantly realized what must have happened when she'd shown up with a baby?

Finally, he told himself to stop. Yes, he'd been wrong to assume that Gabby's connection with Brock had been romantic and consensual. As memories came back to him, he had to acknowledge that Brock had always been hostile to him, had always wanted what Reese had—the grades, the athletic success, the friends. And yes, he'd been jealous of Reese's close connection with Gabby.

One of the few physical fights they'd ever had

had been because of remarks Brock had made about Gabby, insinuating that, of course, a poor girl from a bad family would readily be intimate with any boy.

He shook away the thoughts that were threatening to undo him. Talk about a bad family. Yes, Gabby had faced a lot of difficulty and heartbreak at the hands of her mother, and she hadn't known her father. But her grandmother had stepped up and made a warm and wonderful home for Gabby, and as a result, she'd become a strong and resourceful person.

Whereas Reese himself...

Reese had started out with a strong family, but the years of putdowns from his aunt and uncle, both open and subtle, had taken their toll. He'd come to doubt himself, to agree with their assessment that there was something inherently flawed about him.

That was why he'd been so quick to assume the worst about Gabby. Because he hadn't felt worthy of a woman like her. On some level he'd been waiting for rejection, both when he'd gone overseas and when they'd connected again.

But when he remembered to let the fullness of God's love live inside him, he remembered that his worth wasn't based on any human assessment, nor on what he'd done right or wrong. He was a child of God, and that made him worthy. Just as Gabby was worthy.

But he still wanted to set right the wrong he'd done her. He pulled up to his aunt and uncle's home—the mansion that had never felt like home to him, even though he'd lived there throughout middle and high school—took a couple of deep breaths to remind himself to stay cool and headed for the front door.

The lawn decorations were all restored, he noted.

Uncle Clive had turned down Reese's offer to help with it, saying the gardener would take care of it, which he obviously had.

He tapped lightly on the door and then walked inside. The Christmas tree in the foyer was perfectly decorated in silver and gold, and the even bigger tree in the front room was also perfectly decorated, this one in shades of blue and purple, presumably to match the furniture.

He thought of the lopsided tree in Gabby's grandmother's living room, bearing all colors of cheap ornaments mingled in with Gabby's preschool creations and strings of popcorn. Their nativity scene was from one of Nana's ceramic phases and was clearly an amateur production. There was no comparison with his aunt's crystal nativity, painstakingly collected over the years, one expensive piece at a time.

Warm color versus cold ice.

He followed the sound of a TV show into the den. "Hey, the door was unlocked so I walked in." Of course he'd called first; they hated unexpected visitors.

Uncle Clive muted the television. "Welcome, welcome," he said, rising to shake his hand. "What brings you out again on Christmas Eve? You wanted to talk to us about something?"

"That's right." Reese greeted his aunt and bent to kiss the cheek she presented, then sank down onto the ottoman, facing them both. "I want to talk to you both about dropping charges against Jacob."

"We most certainly will not," Aunt Catherine snapped. "That boy needs to be taught a lesson. Maybe if he gets in enough trouble here, he'll leave town for good."

"Is that the goal, really?" Reese tried to keep his

tone of voice mild. "He'll do better here than he would with his father, it seems."

"Not our problem." Aunt Catherine brushed her hands together as if washing away unpleasant dirt. "We raised our son well. If other people can't do that, then they should bear the penalty. Not God-fearing citizens like us."

Reese's eyes narrowed. The way they'd raised Brock had made him the entitled, bullying person he'd become. The *criminal* he'd become.

Reese faced them down. "You definitely don't want to hurt this family. They've been through enough at our hands. At *Brock's* hands."

He expected questions, was prepared to explain as much as was required to get them to leave Jacob alone. But instead of responding to his statement with surprise, his aunt and uncle glanced at each other.

"Reese is right," Uncle Clive said. "It's Christmas! We should let the boy off the hook."

Aunt Catherine's eyes narrowed. "That whole family is appalling. I don't want them in my town."

"Catherine…" Uncle Clive's tone held a warning.

Shock made Reese forget caution. "You *know*," he blurted out.

"Know what?" Uncle Clive asked, his voice bland.

"You know what Brock did."

His aunt began blustering. "There are so many ways to interpret things," and "no one knows what actually happened," and "Brock was a good boy."

Reese barely heard her words. His world was shifting. He'd always thought of his aunt and uncle as difficult but basically good people; after all, they'd taken him in and given him a home when he'd had nowhere else to go.

But if they'd known what Brock did… "When my cousin was in the accident," he asked his uncle, speaking slowly, "did you speak with him before he passed away?"

Uncle Clive didn't answer.

"Yes," his aunt choked out. "We were able to say goodbye. Talk to him about heaven."

"Catherine…" Again, his uncle's tone held a warning.

"What was said is between us." She looked at the two of them, her eyebrows drawn together, face flushed. "I blame that girl for his death."

"You *what*?" Reese stared at the woman who'd helped raise him, whom he'd thought he'd known. "You know what he did, and you're blaming *her*?"

The implications of that were so big that he couldn't begin to fathom them. If the police had been notified…if there'd been an investigation…at a minimum, Brock's parents would have been required to give Gabby child support for Izzy.

She'd suffered so much. She'd had to be so strong, and it broke his heart. Roused his anger, too, and his fist clenched, but he forced himself to relax.

This was in God's hands. It wasn't up to Reese to bring out what had happened, at least not without consulting Gabby. Enough of her power had been stolen from her in that act of violence. She didn't need him to orchestrate what happened next.

When and whether the truth came out was her decision, and knowing Gabby, he had no doubt she'd thought about how much of the circumstances of her conception to reveal to Izzy when she was old enough to hear it.

Should his aunt and uncle admit the truth and possibly be allowed to be Izzy's grandparents?

His own impulse was to say "no way." They'd proven themselves to be bad parents.

He had to wonder, though, whether they'd looked at Izzy and seen their son, as Reese had, as Marla had, and maybe as others had, as well.

He looked from his aunt to his uncle, both of whom were watching him.

"Will you drop charges against Jacob?" he asked.

Uncle Clive nodded immediately.

Aunt Catherine opened and closed her mouth a couple of times, looking anywhere but at Reese.

"Catherine," Uncle Clive said. "It's the right thing to do. We were wrong to come down on him so hard before, for his friendship with Paige."

She sucked in a breath, then let it out, seeming to deflate at the same time. "Oh, all right."

Reese nodded, stood, and turned to leave.

"Wait, Reese." Aunt Catherine sounded almost desperate. "Are you coming for Christmas dinner tomorrow? We're having several couples over and we'd love to have you join us."

To fill the gap in their lives? To impress their friends with a wounded veteran, now that that was trendy?

"No," he said. "I have other plans." He strode out the door, ignoring his aunt sputtering behind him.

He had a lot to do before tomorrow, and not much time in which to do it.

Chapter Fifteen

In the predawn dark of Christmas morning, Gabby checked on the peacefully sleeping Izzy, washed her face and went downstairs. She stirred flour together with yeast and salt, then heated milk, butter and sugar in a small saucepan. She tested the temperature, then stirred the liquid mixture into the dry one, gradually beating in an egg and more flour. Once the dough looked the same as Nana's, or almost, she placed it on the flour-covered counter and started to knead.

Worries about Jacob crowded in, but she firmly pushed all her disasterizing thoughts aside. She'd prayed the situation into God's hands and there was no more she could do.

Thinking of Jacob took her back to two nights ago, to the Markowskis' house. To thoughts of Brock.

Remembering him, seeing the image of his face and smile, had shaken her...but it hadn't broken her. The assault was a trauma she'd never forget, but after so many prayers, so many tears, she'd moved beyond it. She had a real life to live now, a daughter to raise. Brock had paid for his crime, the ultimate price, and he, too, was in God's hands now, to be dealt with as God willed. Searching her heart, she found that most of the hatred she'd felt for him had faded away.

And that left Reese. He'd apologized for his lack of belief in her last night. She was glad of that, because part of her wanted him to think well of her. He'd been so important in her emotional life for so long.

And yet she couldn't trust his words; or rather, they weren't enough. He'd declared love for her before, told her he wanted to spend the rest of his life with her, begged her to wait for him. But with just one social media posting, his perception of her had changed, and his feelings had been too quick to change, too.

He'd been quick to judge her and find her wanting. Quick to anger.

If she'd been on her own, she might have risked accepting his apology, smiling sweetly, trying again.

But she had Nana, and Jacob and most of all Izzy to care for. She had to take care of herself so she could take care of them. Put on her oxygen mask first, just like she'd heard they instructed on an airplane, not that she'd ever been on one.

Whatever Reese thought of her, whatever the Markowskis thought of her didn't matter. She knew now, inside herself, that she was an okay person and she was going to do okay. Her mistakes and sins were forgiven, and she was loved by God.

As the sun rose, making diamonds on the snow, she felt glad to be staying here, in the town where she'd grown up, where her family was. Here, she could help Jacob and Nana, and she could raise Izzy.

She checked the dough. It had risen just enough, so she turned it onto the floury counter and rolled it out into a rectangle, the long motions of Nana's old rolling pin soothing her. She'd wanted to make Izzy's first Christmas special, but there would be no frilly dress, no shiny baby toys, no board or bathtub books. Not this year. Nana was fine about the lack of gifts, of course, but Jacob would be disappointed that she was going to have to return his hockey stick and skates so she could pay the Markowskis for his vandalism. It was a valid consequence, but a tough lesson to learn at fifteen.

She painted melted butter onto the dough and then sprinkled a mixture of cinnamon and brown sugar generously over the whole thing.

Christmas wasn't about gifts; it was about Jesus. Through tears, as she rolled and then sliced the cinnamon-filled log, she lifted her praises and thanks.

But after sharing her joy with God, she had to share the sorrow that had caused the tears. How she'd wanted a complete family, wanted to be loved in the special way that a husband loved a wife. Wanted to be someone's favorite person, wanted to make someone's eyes light up.

She'd *wanted* it to be Reese. Wanted it with all her heart, and she could share that, now, with God.

Not my will but Thine, she whispered as she slid the cinnamon rolls into the oven.

The spicy, yeasty smell of them brought Jacob downstairs first, and he actually came over to the kitchen table where Gabby was sitting and gave her a quick hug. "Merry Christmas, sis," he said.

"Same to you, kiddo." She bit her lip. "I'm not going to be able to give you a present."

"I figured," he said, sounding philosophical. "Whatever you're baking will do just fine for me."

Inspiration struck. She couldn't give him a physical

gift, but she could give him something that might be even better. "Jacob," she said, putting into words the plan she'd been pondering, "would you like to stay here?"

His head whipped around to face her. "What do you mean?"

"Stay here permanently. With me, and Nana and Izzy."

"Even after what I did?"

She shrugged. "We're family. When we make mistakes, we still love each other."

The words hung in the air as they looked at each other, and then Jacob rubbed a knuckle across his face. "Something in my eye," he mumbled. "Is Nana okay with it?"

"Okay with what?" Nana said through a yawn. She stood in the doorway in her old chenille bathrobe, holding Izzy, who was bundled in a blanket and babbling long strings of nonsense syllables in the rising and falling tones of a meaningful conversation.

"With Jacob staying here," Gabby said.

"I'd like nothing better. And what's more, I think I can talk your father into it." Nana walked over to squeeze Jacob's shoulder. "But we can have no repeats of what you did at the Markowskis' place, understand?"

"I understand. I'm sorry for all the trouble I caused." He gave Nana a quick, fierce hug.

Feeling teary herself, Gabby enlisted Jacob to frost the cinnamon rolls while she ran upstairs to throw on jeans and her old red sweater. And then they gathered around the table, and prayed and ate together.

It was enough. It had to be.

This hole in her heart would heal. Eventually.

Gabby had just started dishing out a second round of rolls when the doorbell rang.

Jacob's mouth was full and Nana was holding a new sippy cup for Izzy, so Gabby went to answer the door. At first, all she could see was a white beard and hair and red Santa suit. And bags. Lots and lots of bags, overflowing from Santa's arms onto Nana's porch.

"Ho ho ho!" came a deep voice.

She'd recognize it anywhere. "Reese?" She just stared, trying to figure out what she was seeing and hearing.

"Can you let a merry old guy in?"

"Um...sure, I guess." She held the door wider.

His costume made him almost too broad for the doorway, but he pushed his way in, eyes twinkling above a cottony beard.

"Let me help you, um, Santa," she said, and took the packages from his arms. *What on earth?* He turned to grab more bags: wrapped presents, what looked like colorful decorations, and groceries—a large ham, a couple of pies, dishes of vegetables and potatoes.

As soon as they'd carried everything into the kitchen, Reese knelt down low in front of Izzy, speaking softly. "Ho ho ho," he said, dangling a stuffed reindeer. "I hear it's somebody's first Christmas."

She laughed and reached for it.

"And I think you'd look awfully pretty in a new dress." He held up a stretchy red one and then pulled a bright red snowsuit from another bag.

Gabby snapped pictures and cried.

As Reese helped clean up the wrapping paper after they'd feasted and opened gifts, he looked over at Gabby. She was squatting in front of Izzy, holding out her arms, trying to encourage Izzy to let go of the sofa and walk to her.

It wasn't happening yet, but it would surely be soon.

Whether his relationship with Gabby would move forward similarly was anyone's guess.

He couldn't find out unless he could get her alone, and that wasn't going to be easy. He knelt beside Nana's recliner. "I need your help," he said, and explained what he wanted to do.

Minutes later, she'd collected Izzy and Jacob and gone upstairs with promises of an Xbox marathon and a nap.

Gabby looked after them like she wanted to follow, so he took her hand. "I need to talk to you a minute," he said, and drew her toward the Christmas tree.

"Oh! Of course." She shook her head and pulled her hand away. "In all the excitement I forgot to thank you. You did a very kind thing today."

"I had a lot to make up for," he said, facing her. "I was wrong, Gabby. I jumped to conclusions, I guess because I'm insecure in certain ways. I didn't think someone like you would really want me, and I made that come true."

She crossed her arms and studied him, head cocked to one side.

"Because of this, partly," he said, holding up his prosthesis.

"Oh, Reese. That means nothing to me, except that you sacrificed for the rest of us."

"Partly also because of…other things."

"Your uncle and aunt?"

He nodded, then clapped his hand to his forehead.

"I forgot to tell you! They're not going to press charges against Jacob."

Her eyes widened. "You talked them out of it?"

"Yeah." He'd tell her the whole story later; she deserved to know. But right now, he had something else he wanted to do.

She wrapped her arms around him in a sudden tight hug that took his breath. And then she let go and backed away just as quickly. "Can we go tell Jacob? I know it was weighing on him today."

He was never going to get another chance like this. "In a few minutes," he said. "I have something I want to discuss with you first."

"But knowing Jacob isn't in trouble...it's the best Christmas gift ever! Thank you so, so much."

"I have another one," he said. Sinking down on one knee, he reached into his pocket and pulled out the little box that he'd had for three plus years. He'd never thought he'd get the chance to make this offer, but it was time. Past time.

"I love you, Gabby. I've loved you since the first time I kissed you on Romano's Mountain. You're beautiful, and amazing, and kind and smart, and...will you marry me?"

Gabby pinched the skin on the back of her hand to figure out whether she was dreaming.

It hurt. She wasn't.

Will you marry me? He'd really said it.

But did he mean it? Was it as changeable as his teenage feelings of love for her, easily destroyed by something somebody said?

Be still. It was a piece of one of her favorite Bible

verses, and she'd found it more and more applicable as she'd assumed the hectic life of a single working mom. Once she stilled her mind, the day's reality had room to come in.

He'd shown up in a Santa suit and brought gifts for all of them, including a little Christmas outfit for Izzy that made her look like a Christmas elf. That meant he remembered Gabby's offhand comment that she wanted to buy Izzy a Christmas outfit. Remembered it and noticed that it hadn't happened yet.

Dressed in that uncomfortable rented Santa suit, he'd stood still for photo after photo. And then he'd helped them cook the Christmas dinner he'd brought fixings for, ate it with them, talking and laughing like a member of the family, and then helped clean up.

And he'd gotten Jacob off the hook with his aunt and uncle.

He'd been so kind to all of them. He seemed to genuinely care for Jacob and for Nana, which meant he could truly be a part of their family. He'd gone beyond words into actions, which was priceless to her.

But she had one more worry before she could relax into what Reese seemed to be offering. "Wait here," she said, patting the couch. And then she rushed upstairs. "I need to borrow Izzy," she said to Nana. She picked up the baby. Held her close and breathed in her sweet fragrance.

She loved Reese with all her heart; she could admit that now. Maybe she'd never stopped loving him.

But now, she loved Izzy that much and more, and she had a responsibility.

She carried Izzy over to the couch where Reese was sitting, and this time it was she who went to her knees, a posture of supplication consciously chosen. "We're a package deal, Reese," she said, holding Izzy snug against her. "She's my joy out of sorrow, and she's…" She swallowed, then made herself say it. "She's Brock's child by blood. Can you accept her, knowing that?"

The Christmas lights shone behind him, and the smell of evergreens was heavy in the air as he met her eyes. Deliberately, he held out his arms for Izzy and then cuddled her close, just as Gabby had. "How can I not accept her," he asked, "when she's a part of you? And when you're such a wonderful mother to her, even after all you went through?" He placed a resounding kiss on the top of Izzy's head, and she laughed up at him, so sweet and trusting.

Seeing the two of them together, Gabby's eyes filled.

"I want to be a father to her," Reese said, looking back at Gabby.

She opened her mouth to tell him she'd marry him tomorrow, but he held up a hand. "I know I've made mistakes," he said. "If you can't say yes now, it's okay, just…just please don't close the door entirely if there's even a chance."

She felt her lips curve into a watery smile. Yes, Reese had made some mistakes, but so had she. She'd readily forgive him if he could forgive her. She climbed up onto the couch right next to him. "I'd love to marry you," she said, "because I love you. I think I always have."

His face lit up and he wrapped his arms around her. "I love you so much," he said.

With those words, all the acceptance she'd desired

burst over her like fireworks, and all the hurt she'd felt as a neglected kid and as a victim of assault dissolved in the warmth of Reese's embrace.

As she lifted her face to kiss him, she thanked God, who'd orchestrated all of it.

"And…that's a wrap!" came Jacob's voice minutes later. "Come on, guys, enough kissing already!"

Gabby reluctantly pulled away from Reese and turned. There was Jacob marching into the room, obviously pleased with himself. Nana was right behind him, a huge smile breaking her face into a million happy wrinkles.

"I caught it all on video," Jacob said. "Nice proposal, dude. A little low-key, compared to how some of the guys ask girls to dances, but hey. Whatever works."

"Especially the part with Izzy," Nana declared. "That's going to bring some tears at your wedding."

Gabby looked up at Reese, half laughing, half crying, and gestured toward Jacob and Nana. "Package deal, remember? They're part of the package, too."

"Package deal," he said with a smile. "They're part of who you are. I love you, and I love them, too."

And as they all collapsed onto the couch together, hugging and laughing, Gabby looked heavenward and thanked God for the good and generous gifts He'd given her.

Epilogue

The tulips and daffodils were just starting to poke their heads through the year's last snowfall when Gabby, Reese, Jacob and Nana gathered at the barn minutes before Izzy's first birthday party.

They weren't the first to arrive; several of the Rescue Haven boys were there ahead of them, finalizing the decorations.

The group had insisted on it. They'd been around Izzy so much by now that they mostly thought of her as a little sister. The streamers, posters and balloons looked a bit haphazard; even Paige's influence couldn't tame a whole group of boys who'd wanted to help.

Now more of the boys were drifting in, most of them bringing a parent or relative, since everyone was getting more involved with the Rescue Haven program.

Mr. Romano even showed up, and Gabby glanced over at Reese. "Hope you don't mind that I invited him."

He shook his head. "Nope. Great idea."

Nana was carrying a birthday cake to put on the table and she practically dropped it when she saw Mr.

Romano. "My lands," she said, "I never thought I'd see you in this place."

"I just wanted to see where my money has been going."

"Well, you might as well roll up your sleeves and help me set up this table," Nana ordered.

Gabby was just grateful that Nana was feeling so much better. She was restored to her former state of health and feistiness, and judging from the way Mr. Romano hurried to do her bidding as she bustled around the barn, he liked the change, too.

Corbin was here, and Hannah, and several other friends from church. Of course, Izzy was too little to know what it was all about, but Gabby thought she felt more secure and more loved than ever before, now that they were settled in the community and Reese was playing a more active role in the family.

Now he was lighting the single birthday candle, and she hurried to snap a picture. As they all sang, she let him tug her close.

"We'd better keep an eye on Jacob and Paige," she said. The two youngsters were sitting side by side on a hay bale, looking at a phone and laughing together.

"They're good kids. And I think Aunt Catherine and Uncle Clive are lightening up on Paige. They'll never be thrilled with her dating Jacob, but they've learned that crucial skill of keeping their mouths shut."

Just like they'd kept their mouths shut about what they'd learned from their son. After Reese had told her they'd known about the assault and never spoken up, she'd addressed it with her counselor. With her help, Gabby had had a difficult conversation with the older couple. As of now, Gabby didn't want them to know

Izzy, and they seemed to want to keep everything under wraps, too, watching their grandchild grow from afar; in fact, they were talking about moving to Arizona when Paige graduated.

It was their loss. Gabby wasn't going to spend time worrying, or raging or hurting because of things Mr. and Mrs. Markowski had done wrong.

Through it all, Reese had been a rock of support. He'd never interfered with what she wanted to do and never even made a pointed suggestion; he just listened, and held her and told her she was doing well.

It was a balm to Gabby's heart, being with him, and she thanked God every day for the blessing Reese was to her and Izzy.

Still, if Izzy grew up and wanted to know Brock's parents, if they were still around, they'd reopen the issue. And they'd work with the counselor about how to tell Izzy about her father.

They sang "Happy Birthday" to Izzy and passed out cake, and Gabby thought she couldn't possibly be happier. As Izzy toddled around with help from the various guests, Gabby and Reese watched, arms around each other.

"You know," he said, "I'm really enjoying this fatherhood thing. Do you think…" He trailed off. "Never mind. It's too soon."

"What?" she asked, curious.

"Sure you want to know?"

"I always want to know what's going on in your head," she said.

He tightened his arm around her. "I'm just thinking," he said, "that after we've been married a little while, I wouldn't mind having another child. If you'd like that," he added quickly. "I think Izzy would be a terrific big sister."

"I think she would, too." The idea of having a child with Reese—of having his support throughout the pregnancy, of a joyous birth with a loving husband beside her, of being surrounded by friends and family—made tears spring to Gabby's eyes.

"I'd love having a child with you," she said, and kissed him.

* * * * *

Look for more Rescue Haven books
by Lee Tobin McClain, coming in 2020!

Dear Reader,

Thank you for reading book one in my new Rescue Haven series. Since I love dogs and have a heart for at-risk kids, the Rescue Haven program was really fun for me to write…especially since it takes place at Christmastime, where sledding and church pageants and visits from Santa add to the fun.

The assault Gabby endured, her lonely pregnancy and the initial harsh judgments made by Reese and others are the darker side of this particular story. Darkness is part of life, but how fortunate we are to know a God who can bring joy out of sorrow. Izzy is the wonderful blessing that emerges from the pain of Gabby's past.

If you felt there was a little extra emotion in the portrayal of the senior dog Bundi, you are right. Bundi is modeled on my sister's dog. She's fifteen years old and needs a little extra help navigating the world these days, but she still loves biscuits, belly rubs and everyone she meets. We could all learn a thing or two from Bundi!

Wishing you a very happy Christmas,
Lee

AVAILABLE THIS MONTH FROM
Love Inspired®

AN AMISH CHRISTMAS PROMISE
Green Mountain Blessings • by Jo Ann Brown
Carolyn Wiebe will do anything to protect her late sister's children from their abusive father—even give up her Amish roots and pretend to be Mennonite. But when she starts falling for Amish bachelor Michael Miller, can they conquer their pasts—and her secrets—by Christmas to build a forever family?

COURTING THE AMISH NANNY
Amish of Serenity Ridge • by Carrie Lighte
Embarrassed by an unrequited crush, Sadie Dienner travels to Maine to take a nanny position for the holidays. But despite her vow to put romance out of her mind, the adorable little twins and their handsome Amish father, Levi Swarey, soon have her wishing for love.

THE RANCHER'S HOLIDAY HOPE
Mercy Ranch • by Brenda Minton
Home to help with his sister's wedding, Max St. James doesn't plan to stay past the holidays. With wedding planner Sierra Lawson pulling at his heartstrings, though, he can't help but wonder if the small town he grew up in is right where he belongs.

THE SECRET CHRISTMAS CHILD
Rescue Haven • by Lee Tobin McClain
Back home at Christmastime with a dark secret, single mom Gabby Hanks needs a job—and working at her high school sweetheart's program for at-risk kids is the only option. Can she and Reese Markowski overcome their past...and find a second chance at a future together?

HER COWBOY TILL CHRISTMAS
Wyoming Sweethearts • by Jill Kemerer
The last people Mason Fanning expects to find on his doorstep are his ex-girlfriend Brittany Green and the identical twin he never knew he had. Could this unexpected Christmas reunion bring the widower and his little boy the family they've been longing for?

STRANDED FOR THE HOLIDAYS
by Lisa Carter
All cowboy Jonas Stone's little boy wants for Christmas is a mother. So when runaway bride AnnaBeth Cummings is stranded in town by a blizzard, the local matchmakers are sure she'd make the perfect wife and mother. But can they convince the city girl to fall for the country boy?

LIATMBPA1219

COMING NEXT MONTH FROM
Love Inspired®

Available December 17, 2019

FINDING HER AMISH LOVE
Women of Lancaster County • by Rebecca Kertz
Seeking refuge from her abusive foster father at an Amish farm, Emma Beiler can't tell anyone that she's former Amish whose family was shunned. She's convinced they'd never let her stay. But as love blossoms between her and bachelor Daniel Lapp, can it survive their differences—and her secrets?

THE AMISH MARRIAGE BARGAIN
by Marie E. Bast
May Bender dreamed of marrying Thad Hochstedler—until he jilted her for her sister with no explanation. Now, with Thad widowed and a single father, the bishop insists they conveniently wed for the baby girl. When May learns the real reason for his first marriage, can they rediscover their love?

A HOPEFUL HARVEST
Golden Grove • by Ruth Logan Herne
On the brink of losing her apple orchard after a storm, single mom Libby Creighton can't handle the harvest alone. Reclusive Jax McClaren might be just what her orchard—and her heart—needs. But he's hiding a painful secret past...and love is something he's not quite sure he can risk.

HER SECRET ALASKAN FAMILY
Home to Owl Creek • by Belle Calhoune
When Sage Duncan discovers she was kidnapped as a baby, she heads to a small Alaskan town to learn about her birth family—without disclosing her identity. But as she falls for Sheriff Hank Crawford, revealing the truth could tear them apart...

SNOWBOUND WITH THE COWBOY
Rocky Mountain Ranch • by Roxanne Rustand
Returning home to open a veterinary clinic, the last person Sara Branson expects to find in town is Tate Langford—the man she once loved. Tate is home temporarily, and his family and hers don't get along. So why can't she stop wishing their reunion could turn permanent?

A RANCHER TO TRUST
by Laurel Blount
Rebel turned rancher Dan Whitlock is determined to prove he's a changed man to the wife he abandoned as a teen...but Bailey Quinn is just as set on finally ending their marriage. When tragedy lands Dan as the guardian of little orphaned twins, can he give Bailey all the love—and family—she's ever wanted?

———————

LOOK FOR THESE AND OTHER LOVE INSPIRED BOOKS WHEREVER BOOKS ARE SOLD, INCLUDING MOST BOOKSTORES, SUPERMARKETS, DISCOUNT STORES AND DRUGSTORES.

LICNM1219

"You won't have to stay on our account, and we can look after Ernest's place, too. I can hire a man to help me. Someone I know I can…" Ruth's words trailed away.

Trust? Depend on? Was that what Ruth was going to say? She didn't want him around. She couldn't have made it any clearer. Maybe it had been a mistake to think he could patch things up between them, but he wasn't willing to give up after only one day. Ruth was nothing if not stubborn, but he could be stubborn, too.

Owen leaned back and chuckled.

"What's so funny?"

"I'm here until Ernest returns, Ruth. You can't get rid of me with a few well-placed insults."

She huffed and turned her back to him. "I didn't insult you."

"Ah, but you wanted to. I'd like to talk about my plans in the morning."

Ruth nodded. "You know my feelings, but I agree we both need to sleep on it."

Owen picked up his coat and hat, and left for his uncle's farm. The wind was blowing harder and the snow was piling up in growing drifts. It wasn't a fit night out for man nor beast. As if to prove his point, he found Meeka, Ernest's big guard dog, lying across the corner of the porch out of the wind. Instead of coming out to greet him, she whined repeatedly.

He opened the door of the house. "Come in for a bit." She didn't get up. Something was wrong. Was she hurt? He walked toward her. She sat up and growled low in her throat. She had never done that to him before. "Are you sick, girl?"

She looked back at something in the corner and whined softly. Over the wind he heard what sounded like a sobbing child. "What have you got there, Meeka? Let me see."

He came closer. There was a child in an Amish bonnet and bulky winter coat trying to bury herself beneath Meeka's thick fur. Where had she come from? Why was she here? He looked around. Where were her parents?

Don't miss
The Hope *by Patricia Davids,*
available now wherever
HQN™ books and ebooks are sold.

HQNBooks.com

PHPDEXP1219

Get 4 FREE REWARDS!

We'll send you 2 FREE Books plus 2 FREE Mystery Gifts.

Love Inspired® books feature contemporary inspirational romances with Christian characters facing the challenges of life and love.

FREE
Value Over
$20

It couldn't be.

Ice filled Ashley Willis's veins despite the spring sunshine streaming through the living room windows of the Bristle Township home in Colorado where she rented a bedroom.

Disbelief cemented her feet to the floor, her gaze riveted to the horrific images on the television screen.

Flames shot out of the two-story building she'd hoped never to see again. Its once bright red awnings were now singed black and the magnificent stained glass windows depicting the image of an angry bull were no more.

She knew that place intimately.

The same place that haunted her nightmares.

The newscaster's words assaulted her. She grabbed on to the back of the faded floral couch for support.

"In a fiery inferno, the posh Burbank restaurant The Matador was consumed by a raging fire in the wee hours of the morning. Firefighters are working diligently to douse the flames. So far there have been no fatalities. However, there has been one critical injury."

Ashley's heart thumped painfully in her chest, reminding her to breathe. Concern for her friend Gregor, the man who had safely spirited her away from the Los Angeles area one frightening night a year and a half ago when she'd witnessed her boss, Maksim Sokolov, kill a man, thrummed through her. She had to know what happened. She had to know if Gregor was the one injured.

She had to know if this had anything to do with her.

"Mrs. Marsh," Ashley called out. "Would you mind if I use your cell phone?"

Her landlady, a widow in her mideighties, appeared in the archway between the living room and kitchen. Her hot-pink tracksuit hung on her stooped shoulders, but it was her bright smile that always tugged at Ashley's heart. The woman was a spitfire, with her blue-gray hair and her kind green eyes behind thick spectacles.

"Of course, dear. It's in my purse." She pointed to the black satchel on the dining room table. "Though you know, as I keep saying, you should get your own cell phone. It's not safe for a young lady to be walking around without any means of calling for help."

They had been over this ground before. Ashley didn't want anything attached to her name.

Or rather, her assumed identity—Jane Thompson.

Don't miss
Secret Mountain Hideout *by Terri Reed,*
available January 2020 wherever
Love Inspired Suspense books and ebooks are sold.

LoveInspired.com